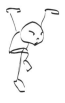

NICOTEXT

NICOS
Cult MovieQuoteBook

NICOTEXT

It is the authors honest and sincere wish that this book will lead to an increased interest in film. We would also like to express our deepest gratitude towards filmproduction-companies, scriptwriters and actors. Without them this book would not excist.

If you find any wrongly quoted movies, or other mistakes PLEASE contact us and we will correct it in the next edition.

Respectfully, NICOTEXT

Fredrik Colting
Carl-Johan Gadd
Stefan Sjölander

©2004 NICOTEXT
info@nicotext.com

Printed by: WS Bookwell, Finland. 2004

ISBN 91-974396-3-0

www.nicotext.com

"-I must be crazy to be in a loony bin like this."

ONE FLEW OVER THE CUCKOO'S NEST

Play the moviequiz game!

Rules:
There are six moviequotes on every right page.
The answers are on the following left page.
Use a dise and guess which movie the quotes are from.
Read one page each and pass the book on.
Note points on a piece of paper.
Play alone or with your friends!

1. "-I haven't got a brain... only straw.
   -How can you talk if you haven't got a brain?
   -I don't know... But some people without brains
   do an awful lot of talking...don't they?
   -Yes, I guess you're right."

2. "-It had been a wonderful evening and what I needed now,
   to give it the perfect ending, was a little of the Ludwig Von."

3. "-We're gonna need a bigger boat."

4. "-It's got a cop motor, a 440 cubic inch plant, it's got cop tires,
   cop suspensions, cop shocks. It's a model made before catalytic
   converters so it'll run good on regular gas. What do you say,
   is it the new Bluesmobile or what?
   -Fix the cigarette lighter."

5. "-When a man is chasing a woman through an alley with
   a butcher's knife and a hard-on, I figure he isn't out collecting
   for the Red Cross!"

6. "-I don't give a good fuck what you know or don't know,
   I'm going to torture you anyway."

1. THE WIZARD OF OZ
1939, USA
Director: Victor Fleming
Actor: Judy Garland, Ray Bolger, Bert Lahr
Script: Noel Langley, Florence Ryerson and Edgar Allan Woolf.
Based on the book by L. Frank Baum.

2. A CLOCKWORK ORANGE
1971, USA
Director: Stanley Kubrick
Actor: Malcolm McDowell, Patrick Magee, Adrienne Corri.
Script: Stanley Kubrick. Based on the book by Anthony Burgess.

3. JAWS
1975, USA
Director: Steven Spielberg
Actor: Roy Scheider, Robert Shaw, Richard Dreyfuss
Script: Peter Benchley, Carl Gottlieb, John Milius, Howard Sackler
and Robert Shaw. Based on the book by Peter Benchley

4. THE BLUES BROTHERS
1980, USA
Director: John Landis
Actor: John Belushi, Dan Aykroyd, Cap Calloway.
Script: Dan Aykroyd and John Landis.

5. DIRTY HARRY
1971, USA
Director: Don Siegal
Actor: Clint Eastwood, Harry Guardino, Reni Santoni.
Script: Harry Julian Fink, Rita M. Fink, Dean Riesner and John Milius.

6. RESERVOIR DOGS
1992, USA
Director: Quentin Tarantino
Actor: Harvey Keitel, Tim Roth, Michael Madsen.
Script: Roger Avary and Quentin Tarantino.

1. "-You call yourself a free spirit, a wild thing, and you're terrified somebody's gonna stick you in a cage. Well baby, you're already in that cage. You built it yourself. And it's not bounded in the west by Tulip, Texas, or in the east by Somali-land. It's wherever you go. Because no matter where you run, you just end up running into yourself."

2. "-When people think you're dying, they really, really listen to you, instead of just...
   - instead of just waiting for their turn to speak?"

3. "-They'll talk to ya and talk to ya and talk to ya about individual freedom. But they see a free Individual, it's gonna scare 'em."

4. "-I can remember when I was a little boy. My grandmother and I could hold conversations entirely without ever opening our mouths."

5. "-If I have any more fun today I don't think I can take it!"

6. "-We got a secret weapon. God is our co-pilot!
   -God is our co-pilot? Remember our car?
   -Yeah?
   -Two seats!
   -Two seats...?
   -Where's he gonna sit? Where?"

9

ANSWER >

1.   BREAKFAST AT TIFFANY'S
        1961, USA
        Director: Blake Edwards
        Actor: Audrey Hepburn, George Peppard
        Script: Truman Capote, George Axelrod

2.   FIGHT CLUB
        1999, USA
        Director: David Fincher
        Actor: Brad Pitt, Edward Norton, Helena Bonham Carter.
        Script: Jim Uhls. Based on the book by Chuck Palahniuk.

3.   EASY RIDER
        1969, USA
        Director: Dennis Hopper
        Actor: Peter Fonda, Dennis Hopper, Jack Nicholson.
        Script: Peter Fonda, Dennis Hopper and Terry Southern.

4.   THE SHINING
        1980, USA
        Director: Stanley Kubrick
        Actor: Jack Nicholson, Shelley Duvall, Danny Lloyd.
        Script: Stanley Kubrick and Diane Johnson.
        Based on the book by Stephen King.

5.   THE TEXAS CHAINSAW MASSACRE
        1974, USA
        Director: Tobe Hopper
        Actor: Marilyn Burns, Gunner Hansen, Ed Neal.
        Script: Kim Henkel and Tobe Hooper.

6.   THE CANNONBALL RUN
        1981, USA
        DIRECTOR: HAL NEEDHAM
        ACTOR: BURT REYNOLDS, ROGER MOORE, FARRAH FAWCETT.
        SCRIPT: BROCK YATES.

1. "-I can't make out whether you're a
    bloody madman or just half-witted.
    -I have the same problem, sir."

2. "-Is there someone inside you?
    -Sometimes.
    -Who is it?
    -I don't know.
    -Is it Captain Howdy?
    -I don't know.
    -If I ask him to tell me, will you let him answer?
    -No!
    -Why not?
    -I'm afraid."

3. "-How do you explain school to a higher intelligence?"

4. "-This snakeskin jacket symbolizes my individuality
    and belief in personal freedom."

5. "-Look at your algebra book, it looks like it's never
    even been opened!
    -I only use it on special equations"

6. "-More human than human is our motto."

ANSWER >

1.   LAWRENCE OF ARABIA
   1962, UNITED KINGDOM
   Director: David Lean.
   Actor: Peter O'Toole, Alec Guinness, Anthony Quinn.
   Script: T.E. Lawrence, Robert Bolt and Michael Wilson.

2.   EXORCIST, THE
   1973, USA
   Director: William Friedkin.
   Actor: Ellen Burstyn, Max Von Sydow, Linda Blair.
   Script: William Peter Blatty.

3.   E.T THE EXTRA-TERRESTRIAL
   1982, USA
   Director: Steven Spielberg.
   Actor: Dee Wallace, Henry Thomas, Peter Coyote.
   Script: Melissa Mathison.

4.   WILD AT HEART
   1990, USA
   Director: David Lynch.
   Actor: Nicolas Cage, Laura Dern, Diane Ladd.
   Script: David Lynch. Based on the book by Barry Gifford.

5.   ROCK 'N' ROLL HIGH SCHOOL
   1979, USA
   Director: Allan Arkush, Joe Dante
   Actor: P.J Soles, Vincent van Patten, Clint Howard
   Script: Richard Whitley, Russ Dronch

6.   BLADE RUNNER
   1982, USA
   Director: Ridley Scott
   Actor: Harrison Ford, Rutger Hauer, Sean Young
   Script: Hampton Fancher, David Webb Peoples, Roland Kibbee.
   Based on the book by Philip K. Dick.

1. "-John Connor gave me a picture of you once. I didn't know why at the time. It was very old, torn, faded. You were young like you are now. You seemed just a little sad. I used to always wonder what you were thinking at that moment. I memorised every line, every curve. I came across time for you Sarah, I love you, I always have."

2. "-I think someone should just take this city and just... just flush it down the fuckin' toilet."

3. "-I don't think about that much with one shot anymore, Mike. -You have to think about one shot. One shot is what it's all about. A deer's gotta be taken with one shot."

4. "-1,000 British soldiers have been massacred. While I stood here talking peace, a war has started."

5. "-I am not an animal! I am a human being! I am a man!"

6. "-Cherry was right. You're soft, you should have let 'em kill me, 'cause I'm gonna kill you. I'll catch up with ya. I don't know when, but I'll catch up. Every time you turn around, expect to see me, 'cause one time you'll turn around and I'll be there. I'm gonna kill ya, Matt."

ANSWER >

1. THE TERMINATOR
1984, USA
Director: James Cameron
Actor: Arnold Schwartzenegger, Michael Biehn,
Linda Hamilton
Script: James Cameron, Gale Anne Hurd,
William Wisher Jr and Harlan Ellison.

2. TAXI DRIVER
1976, USA
Director: Martin Scorsese
Actor: Robert De Niro, Cybill Shepherd, Harvey Keitel
Script: Paul Schrader.

3. THE DEER HUNTER
1978, USA
Director: Michael Cimino
Actor: Robert De Niro, Christopher Walken, Meryl Streep
Script: Michael Cimino, Louis Garfinkle, Quinn K. Redeker and
Deric Washburn.

4. ZULU
1963, UNITED KINGDOM
Director: Cy Endfield
Actor: Stanley Baker, Jack Hawkins, Ulla Jacobsson
Script: John Prebble, John Prebble and Cy Endfield.

5. THE ELEPHANT MAN
1980, USA
Director: David Lynch
Actor: Anthony Hopkins, John Hurt, Anne Bancroft
Script: Christopher De Vore, Eric Bergren and David Lynch.
Based on the book by Sir Frederick Treves and Ashley Montagu.

6. RED RIVER
1948, USA
Director: Howard Hawks
Actor: John Wayne, Montgomery Clift, Walter Brennan
Script: Borden Chase, Borden Chase and Charles Schnee

1. "-You're not the boss of me, Jack! You're not the king of Dirk! I'm the boss of me! I'm the king of me. I'm Dirk Diggler! I'm the star! It's my big dick and I say when we roll!"

2. "-How do you feel?
   -Fast and loose.
   -In the gut, I mean.
   -Tight, but good."

3. "-Faster than a speeding bullet! More powerful than a locomotive! Able to leap tall buildings with a single bound, the infant of Krypton is now the Man of Steel."

4. "-I just wanna know how one becomes a janitor because Andrew here is very interested in pursuing a career in the custodial arts."

5. "-I can't figure out if you're a detective or a pervert.
   -Well, that's for me to know and you to find out."

6. "-I don't think it's nice, you laughin'. You see, my mule don't like people laughing. He gets the crazy idea you're laughin' at him. Now if you apologize, like I know you're going to, I might convince him that you really didn't mean it."

ANSWER >

1. BOOGIE NIGHTS
    1997, USA
    Director: Paul Thomas Anderson.
    Actor: Mark Wahlberg, Burt Reynolds, Julianne Moore.
    Script: Paul Thomas Anderson

2. THE HUSTLER
    1961, USA
    Director: Robert Rossen
    Actor: Paul Newman, Jackie Gleason, Piper Lauire
    Script: Sidney Carroll and Robert Rossen.
    Based on the book by Walter Tevis.

3. SUPERMAN
    1941, USA
    Director: Dave Fleischer
    Actor: Bud Collyer (voice), Joan Alexander (voice)
    Script: Seymour Kneitel, Joe Shuster

4. THE BREAKFAST CLUB
    1985, USA
    Director: John Hughes
    Actor: Emilio Esteves, Judd Nelson, Molly Ringwald
    Script: John Hughes

5. BLUE VELVET
    1986, USA
    Director: David Lynch
    Actor: Kyle MacLachlan, Isabella Rossellini, Dennis Hopper
    Script: David Lynch

6. A FISTFULL OF DOLLARS
    1964, ITALY
    Director: Sergio Leone
    Actor: Clint Eastwood, Marianne Kand, Gian maria Volonté
    Script: A. Bonzzoni, Victor Andrés Catena

www.nicotext.com

1. "-The 1961 Ferrari 250GT California. Less than a hundred were made. My father spent three years restoring this car.
It is his love, it is his passion.
-It is his fault he didn't lock the garage."

2. "-A man can convince anyone he's somebody else, but never himself."

3. "-Good morning! And in case I don't see you: good afternoon, good evening and good night!"

4. "-Now I don't have to tell you good folks what's been happening in our beloved little town. Sheriff murdered, crops burned, stores looted, people stampeded, and cattle raped. The time has come to act, and act fast. I'm leaving."

5. "-If I was an imitation, a perfect imitation, how would you know it was me?"

6. "-I went to the woods because I wanted to live deliberately, I wanted to live deep and suck out all the marrow of life. To put to rest all that was not life, and not when I had come to die discover that I had not lived."

ANSWER >

1. **FERRIS BUELLER'S DAY OFF**
   1986, USA
   Director: John Hughes
   Actor: Matthew Broderick, Alan Ruck, Mia Sara
   Script: John Hughes

2. **THE USUAL SUSPECTS**
   1995, USA
   Director: Bryan Singer
   Actor: Stephen Baldwin, Gabriel Byrne, Chazz PalMinteri
   Script: Christopher McQuarrie.

3. **THE TRUMAN SHOW**
   1998, USA
   Director: Peter Weir
   Actor: Jim Carrey, Laura Linney, Ed Harris
   Script: Andrew Niccol,

4. **BLAZING SADDLES**
   1973, USA
   Director: Mel Brooks
   Actor: Cleavon Little, Gene Wilder, Harvey Korman
   Script: Andrew Bergman, Mel Brooks, Richard Pryor,
   Norman Steinberg and Alan Uger.

5. **THE THING**
   1982, USA
   Director: John Carpenter
   Actor: Kurt Russell, Richard Dysart, A Wilford Brimley
   Script: John W. Campbell Jr and Bill Lancaster.

6. **DEAD POETS SOCIETY**
   1989, USA
   Director: Peter Weir
   Actor: Robin Williams, Robert Sean Leonard, Ethan Hawke
   Script: Tom Schulman

1. "-Housework is like bad sex. Every time I do it I swear I will never do it again. Until the next time company comes."

2. "-How did you find America?
-Turned left at Greenland."

3. "-Don't you think it would be better if you referred to "it" as "him"?
-If you say so.
-Your compassion's overwhelming, doctor."

4. "-And now, ladies and gentlemen, before I tell you any more, I'm going to show you the greatest thing your eyes have ever beheld. He was a king and a god in the world he knew, but now he comes to civilization merely a captive - a show to gratify your curiosity."

5. "-This is paradise, I'm tellin' ya. This town like a great big pussy jus' waitin' to get fucked."

6. "-I get it. No questions.
-No questions, no lies.
-No questions, no truth, either."

ANSWER >

1. CAN'T STOP THE MUSIC
    1980, USA
    Director: Nancy Walker
    Actor: Alex Briley, David Hodo, Glenn Hughes
    Script: Alan Carr, Bronte Woodard

2. A HARD DAY'S NIGHT
    1964, UNITED KINGDOM
    Director: Richard Lester
    Actor: John Lennon, Paul McCartney, George Harrison
    Script: Alun Owen

3. HALLOWEEN
    1978, USA
    Director: John Carpenter
    Actor: Donald Pleasence, Jamie Lee Curtis, Nancy Loomis
    Script: John Carpenter and Debra Hill.

4. KING KONG
    1976, USA
    Director: John Guillermin
    Actor: Jeff Bridges, Charles Grodin, Jessica Lange
    Script: Merian C. Cooper, Edgar Wallace, James Ashmore Creelman,
    Ruth Rose and Lorenzo Semple Jr.

5. SCARFACE
    1983, USA
    Director: Brian De Palma
    Actor: Al Pacino, Steven Bauer, Michelle Pfeiffer
    Script: Oliver Stone and Howard Hawks.
    Based on the book by Armitage Trail.

6. XANADU
    1980, USA
    Director: Robert Greenwald
    Actor: Olivia Newton John, Gene Kelly, Michael Beck
    Script: Richard Christian Danus and Marc Reid Rubel.

www.nicotext.com

1. "-I see men, sixty, seventy years old breaking their balls to stay fit! What for? When I die, I want to be sick, not healthy."

2. "-Looking at the cake is like looking at the future, until you've tasted it what do you really know? And then, of course, it's too late."

3. "-So, how long you've been in Mexico?
   -A week. I mean a day.
   -Well, which is it? A week or a day?
   -A weekday."

4. "Choose a future .Choose life... But why would I want to do a thing like that? I chose not to choose life, I choose something else. And the reasons? There are no reasons, who needs reasons when you've got heroin."

5. "-There are two kinds of people in this world. Those with loaded guns, and those who dig. You dig."

6. "Remember those posters that said, "Today is the first day of the rest of your life"? Well, that's true of every day but one... The day you die."

ANSWER >

1. THE WITCHES OF EASTWICK
1987, USA
Director: George Miller
Actor: Jack Nicholson, Cher, Susan Sarandon
Script: Michael Cristofer. Based on the book by John Updike.

2. EXCALIBUR
1981, UNITED KINGDOM
Director: John Boorman
Actor: Nicol Williamson, Nigel Terry, Helen Mirren
Script: Rospo Pallenberg and John Boorman.
Based on the book by Thomas Malory.

3. UP IN SMOKE
1978, USA
Director: Lou Adler
Actor: Cheech Marin, Tommy Chong, Stacy Keach
Script: Tommy Chong and Cheech Marin.

4. TRAINSPOTTING
1996, UNITED KINGDOM
Director: Danny Boyle
Actor: Ewan McGregor, Ewan Bremmer, Jonny Lee Miller
Script: John Hodge. Based on the book by Irvine Welsh.

5. THE GOOD, THE BAD, AND THE UGLY
1966, ITALY/SPAIN
Director: Sergio Leone
Actor: Clint Eastwood, Lee Van Cleef, Eli Wallach
Script: Luciano Vincenzoni, Sergio Leone, Agenore Incrocci and
Furio Scarpelli.

6. AMERICAN BEAUTY
1999, USA
Director: Sam Mendes
Actor: Kevin Spacey, Annette Bening, Thora Birch
Script: Alan Ball

www.nicotext.com

1. "-I have existed from the morning of the world and I shall exist until the last star falls from the night. Although I have taken the form of Gaius Caligula, I am all men as I am no man and therefore I am a God."

2. "-I realized my true calling in life.
-What's that?
-Shit, man, I'm a natural born killer."

3. "-I'm not gonna debate you, Jerry.
-Okay.
-I'm not gonna sit here and debate."

4. "-I'm not the Messiah! Will you please listen? I am not the Messiah, do you understand?! Honestly!
-Only the true Messiah denies His divinity.
-What?! Well, what sort of chance does that give me? All right! I am the Messiah!
-He is! He is the Messiah!
-Now, fuck off!
-How shall we fuck off, O Lord?"

5. "-Secret's in the sauce."

6. "-I run a couple of newspapers. What do you do?"

ANSWER >

1.   CALIGULA
     1980, ITALY/USA
     DIRECTOR: TINTO BRASS
     ACTOR: MALCOLM MCDOWELL, PETER O'TOOLE, TERESA ANN SAVOY
     SCRIPT: GORE VIDAL, BOB GUCCIONE, GIANCARLO LUI, MASOLINO D'AMICO,
     FRANCO ROSSELLINI AND ROBERTO ROSSELLINI

2.   NATURAL BORN KILLERS
     1994, USA
     Director: Oliver Stone
     Actor: Woody Harrelson, Juliette Lewis, Robert Downey Jr
     Script: Quentin Tarantino, David Veloz, Richard Rutowski and
     Oliver Stone.

3.   FARGO
     1996, USA
     Director: Joel Coen
     Actor: Francos McDormand, William H Macy, Steve Buscemi
     Script: Joel Coen and Ethan Coen.

4.   MONTY PYTHON'S LIFE OF BRIAN
     1979, UNITED KINGDOM
     Director: Terry Jones
     Actor: Graham Chapman, John Cleese, Terry Gilliam
     Script: Graham Chapman, John Cleese, Terry Gilliam, Eric Idle,
     Terry Jones and Michael Palin.

5.   FRIED GREEN TOMATOES
     1991, USA
     Director: Jon Avnet
     Actor: Kathy Bates, Jessica Tandy, Mary Stuart
     Script: Carol Sobieski, Fannie Flagg.
     Based on the book by Fannie Flagg.

6.   CITIZEN KANE
     1941, USA
     Director: Orson Welles
     Actor: Orson Welles, Joseph Cotten, Everett Sloane
     Script: Herman J. Mankiewicz, Orson Welles and John Houseman.

1. "-We can't go around measuring our goodness by what we don't do, by what we deny ourselves, by what we resist and who we exclude; I think we got to measure goodness by what we embrace, by what we create, and who we enclude."

2. "This here's Miss Bonnie Parker. I'm Clyde Barrow. We rob banks."

3. "-Chief, if I were surrounded by say six or eight of these things, would I stand a chance?
-Well, if you had a gun, shoot 'em in the head. If you didn't, get a torch and burn 'em, they go up pretty easy. Beat 'em or burn 'em."

4. "-Uh-uh, Mother-m-mother, uh, what is the phrase? She isn't quite herself today."

5. "-The only evidence I see of the antichrist here, is everyones desire to see him at work"

6. "-Before he came down here, it never snowed. And afterwards, it did. I don't think it would be snowing now if he weren't still up there. Sometimes you can still catch me dancing in it."

ANSWER >

1. CHOCOLAT
    2000, USA
    Director: Lasse Hallström
    Actor: Johnny Depp, Alfred Molina, Lena Olin
    Script: Robert Nelson Jacobs

2. BONNIE AND CLYDE
    1967, USA
    Director: Arthur Penn
    Actor: Warren Beatty, Faye Dunaway, Michael J Pollard
    Script: David Newman, Robert Benton and Robert Towne.

3. NIGHT OF THE LIVING DEAD
    1968, USA
    Director: George A Romero
    Actor: Duane Jones, Judith O'Dea, Russell Streiner
    Script: George A. Romero and John A. Russo.

4. PSYCHO
    1960, USA
    Director: Alfred Hitchcook
    Actor: Anthony Perkins, Janet Leigh, Vera Miles
    Script: Joseph Stefano. Based on the book by Robert Bland.

5. THE NAME OF THE ROSE
    1986, FRANCE/ITALY/WESTGERMANY
    Director: Jean Jacques Annaud
    Actor: Sean Connery, F Murray Abraham, Christian Slater
    Script: Andrew Birkin, Gérard Brach, Howard Franklin and
    Alain Godard.
    Based on the book by Umberto Eco.

6. EDWARD SCISSORHANDS
    1990, USA
    Director: Tim Burton
    Actor: Johnny Depp, Winona Ryder, Dianne West
    Script: Tim Burton and Caroline Thompson.

1. "-Let me put it this way, Mr. Amer. The 9000 series is the most reliable computer ever made. No 9000 computer has ever made a mistake or distorted information. We are all, by any practical definition of the words, foolproof and incapable of error."

2. "-It's not easy being a cast-iron bitch. It takes discipline, years of training... A lot of people don't appreciate that."

3. "-My style, you can call the art of fighting without fighting."

4. "-Nothing's riding on this except the, uh, first amendment to the Constitution, freedom of the press, and maybe the future of the country. Not that any of that matters, but if you guys fuck up again, I'm going to get mad. Goodnight."

5. "-The Irish are the blacks of Europe. Dubliners are the blacks of Ireland. North Dubliners are the blacks of Dublin."

6. "- If you were mine, I wouldn't share you with anybody or anything. It'd be just you and me. We'd be the center of it all. I know it would feel a lot more like love than being left alone with your work."

ANSWER >

1. 2001: A SPACE ODYSSEY
    1968, UNITED KINGDOM
    Director: Stanley Kubrick
    Actor: Keir Dullea, William Sylvester, Gary Lockwood
    Script: Stanley Kubrick and Arthur C. Clarke.

2. THE ABYSS
    1989, USA
    Director: James Cameron
    Actor: Ed Harris, Mary Elizabeth Mastrantonio, Michael Biehn
    Script: James Cameron

3. ENTER THE DRAGON
    1973, USA
    Director: Robert Clouse
    Actor: Bruce Lee, John Saxon, Jim Kelly
    Script: Michael Allin

4. ALL THE PRESIDENTS MEN
    1976, USA
    Director: Alan J Pakula
    Actor: Robert Redford, Dustin Hoffman, Jason Roberts
    Script: William Goldman. Based on the book by Carl Bernstein and
    Bob Woodward.

5. THE COMMITMENTS
    1991, UNITED KINGDOM
    Director: Alan Parker
    Actor: Robert Arkins, Michael Aherne, Angeline Ball
    Script: Dick Clement, Ian La Frenais and Roddy Doyle.
    Based on the book by Roddy Doyle.

6. REDS
    1981, USA
    Director: Warren Beatty
    Actor: Warren Beatty, Diane Keaton, Edward Herrmann
    Script: Warren Beatty, Trevor Griffiths, Elaine May, John Reed,
    Jeremy Pikser and Peter S. Feibleman.

1. "-I just wish for once that you could be in my shoes, Mr. Prosecutor, and then you would know something that you don't know: mercy! That the concept of a society is based on the quality of that mercy; its sense of fair play; its sense of justice! But I guess that's like asking a bear to shit in the toilet."

2. "-Afraid this tea is pathetic. I must have used those wretched leaves about twenty times. It's not that I mind so much. Tea without milk is so uncivilized."

3. "-Your reality, sir, is lies and balderdash and I'm delighted to say that I have no grasp of it whatsoever."

4. "-The wind whispers of fear and hate. The war has killed love. And those that confess to the Angka are punished, and no one dare ask where they go. Here, only the silent survive."

5. "-If you want me to stop, tell me now.
   -No one's asking you to."

6. "-I've just been to the dedication of the new children's park.
   -Yeah, how did that go?
   -Janice Van Meter got hit with a baseball. It was fabulous.
   -Was she hurt?
   -I doubt it. She got hit in the head."

ANSWER >

1. **MIDNIGHT EXPRESS**
   1978, UNITED KINGDOM
   Director: Alan Parker
   Actor: Brad Davis, Irene Miracle, Bo Hopkins
   Script: Oliver Stone. Based on the book by Billy Hayes and
   William Hoffer.

2. **THE GREAT ESCAPE**
   1962, USA
   Director: John Sturges,
   Actor: Steve McQueen, James Garner, Richard Attenborough
   Script: James Clavell and W.R. Burnett.
   Based on the book by Paul Brickhill.

3. **THE ADVENTURES OF BARON MUNCHAUSEN**
   1989, UNITED KINGDOM
   Director: Terry Gilliam
   Actor: John Neville, Eric Idle, Sarah Polley
   Script: Terry Gilliam and Charles McKeown.
   Based on the book avv Rudolph Erich Raspe. n

4. **THE KILLING FIELDS**
   1984, UNITED KINGDOM
   Director: Roland Joffe
   Actor: Sam Waterston, Haing S Ngor, John Malkovich
   Script: Bruce Robinson

5. **THE BRIDGES OF MADISON COUNTY**
   1995, USA
   Director: Clint Eastwood
   Actor: Clint Eastwood, Meryl Streep, Annie Corley
   Script: Richard LaGravenese.
   Based on the book avRobert James Waller.

6. **STEEL MAGNOLIAS**
   1989, USA
   Director: Herbert Ross
   Actor: Sally Field, Dolly Parton, Julia Roberts
   Script: Robert Harling.

1. "-But Mama, the men she finds. The last one was so
   old and he was bald. He had no hair.
   -A poor girl without a dowry can't be so paticular.
   You want hair, marry a monkey."

2. "-You know something? You read too many comic books."

3. "-This young man has had a very trying rookie season,
   with the litigation, the notoriety, his subsequent deportation
   to Canada and that country's refusal to accept him.
   Number six, Ogie Oglethorpe."

4. "-There are two ways to disable an alligator, Mr. Bond.
   -I don't suppose you'd tell me what they are.
   -One way is to jab a pen right above it's eye.
   -And the other way?
   -Oh, the other way is twice as simple. Just stick your hand in it's
   mouth and pull out all it's teeth. Heh, heh."

5. "-Well, does he make you laugh?
   -He doesnt make me cry."

6. "-Well I wouldn't kick Mick Jagger out of my bed,
   but I'm not a homosexual."

ANSWER >

1. **FIDDLER ON THE ROOF**
   1971, USA
   Director: Norman Jewison
   Actor: (Chaim) Topol, Norma Crane, Leonard Frey
   Script: Joseph Stein. Based on the book by Sholom Aleichem.

2. **REBEL WITHOUT A CAUSE**
   1955, USA
   Director: Nicholas Ray
   Actor: James Dean, Natalie Wood, Sal Mineo
   Script: Nicholas Ray, Irving Shulman and Stewart Stern.

3. **SLAP SHOT**
   1977, USA
   Director: George Roy
   Actor: Paul Newman, Michael Ontkean, Lindsay Crouse
   Script: Nancy Dowd

4. **LIVE AND LET DIE**
   1973, UNITED KINGDOM
   Director: Guy Hamilton
   Actor: Roger Moore, Yaphet Kotto, Jane Seymour
   Script: Tom Mankiewicz. Based on the book by Ian Fleming.

5. **OCEAN'S ELEVEN**
   1960, USA
   Director: Lewis Milestone
   Actor: Frank Sinatra, Dean Martin, Sammy Davis Jr
   Script: George Clayton Johnson, Jack Golden Russell, Harry Brown, Charles Lederer and Billy Wilder.

6. **HAIR**
   1979, USA
   Director: Milos Forman
   Actor: John Savage, Treat Williams, Beverly D'Angelo
   Script: Gerome Ragni, James Rado, Galt MacDermot and Michael Weller.

1. "-Maybe you shouldn't drink so much.
   -Maybe I shouldn't breathe so much either."

2. "-His high exaltedness, the Great Jabba the Hutt,
   has decreed that you are to be terminated immediately.
   -Good, I hate long waits."

3. "-You can turn your back on a person, but don't ever turn your
   back on a drug. Especially when it's waving a razor-sharp hunting
   knife in your eye."

4. "-Men would pay $200 for me, and here you are turning down
   a freebie. You could get a perfectly good dishwasher for that."

5. "-Have you ever seen a Commie drink a glass of water?
   -Well, I can't say I have."

6. "-A lot of holes in the desert, and a lot of problems are buried in
   those holes. But you gotta do it right. I mean, you gotta have the
   hole already dug before you show up with a package in the trunk.
   Otherwise, you're talking about a half-hour to forty-five minutes
   worth of digging. And who knows who's gonna come along in
   that time? Pretty soon, you gotta dig a few more holes.
   You could be there all fuckin' night."

ANSWER >

1. LEAVING LAS VEGAS
    1995, USA
    Director: Mike Figgis
    Actor: Nicolas Cage, Elisabeth Shue, Julian Sands
    Script: Mike Figgis. Based on the book by John O'Brien.

2. RETURN OF THE JEDI
    1983, USA
    Director: Richard Marquand
    Actor: Mark Hamill, Harrison Ford, Carrie Fisher
    Script: George Lucas and Lawrence Kasdan.

3. FEAR AND LOATHING IN LAS VEGAS
    1998, USA
    Director: Terry Gilliam
    Actor: Johnny Depp, Benicio Del Toro, Tobey Maguire
    Script: Terry Gilliam, Tony Grisoni, Tod Davies and Alex Cox.
    Based on the book by Hunter S. Thompson.

4. KLUTE
    1971, USA
    Director: Alan J Pakula
    Actor: Jane Fonda, Donald Sutherland, Charles Cioffi
    Script: Andy Lewis and Dave Lewis .

5. DR STRANGELOVE OR: HOW I LEARNED TO STOP
    WORRYING AND LOVE THE BOMB
    1963, UNITED KINGDOM
    Director: Stanley Kubrick
    Actor: Peter Sellers, George C Scott, Sterling Hayden
    Script: Stanley Kubrick, Terry Southern and Peter George.
    Based on the book by Peter George.

6. CASINO
    1995, USA
    Director: Martin Scorsese
    Actor: Robert De Niro, Sharon Stone Joe Pesci
    Script: Nicholas Pileggi and Martin Scorsese.
    Based on the book by Nicholas Pileggi.

1. "Courage! What makes a king out of a slave? What makes the flag on the mast to wawe? Courage! What makes the elephant charge his tusk in the misty mist, or the dusky dusk? What makes the muskrat guard his musk? Courage! What makes the sphinx the seventh wonder? Courage! What makes the damn come up like thunder? Courage! What makes the Hottentot so hot? What puts the "ape" in apricot? What have they got that I ain't got. -Courage!"

2. "-I don't make things difficult. That's the way they get, all by themselves."

3. "-You're late.
-You're stunning.
-You're forgiven."

4. "-I could have killed 'em all, I could kill you. In town you're the law, out here it's me. Don't push it. Don't push it or I'll give you a war you won't belive."

5. "-I Thought you knew. I want to go throughout life jumping into fountains naked."

6. "-Bring the dog, I love animals... I'm a great cook."

      ANSWER >

1. **THE WIZARD OF OZ**
   1939, USA
   Director: Victor Fleming
   Actor: Judy Garland, Ray Bolger, Bert Lahr
   Script: Noel Langley, Florence Ryerson and Edgar Allan Woolf.
   Based on the book by L. Frank Baum.

2. **LETHAL WEAPON**
   1987, USA
   Director: Richard Donner
   Actor: Mel Gibson, Danny Glover, Gary Busey
   Script: Shane Black

3. **PRETTY WOMAN**
   1990, USA
   Director: Garry Marshall
   Actor: Richard Gere, Julia Roberts, Ralph Bellamy
   Script: J.F Lawton

4. **FIRST BLOOD**
   1982, USA
   Director: Ted Kotcheff
   Actor: Sylvester Stallone, Richard Crenna, Brian Dennehy
   Script: Michael Kozoll, William Sackheim, Sylvester Stallone.
   Based on the book by David Morrell.

5. **THE BIRDS**
   1963, USA
   Director: Alfred Hitchcock
   Actor: Rod Taylor, Tippi Hedren, Jessica Tandy
   Script: Daphne Du Maurier and Evan Hunter.

6. **FATAL ATTRACTION**
   1987, USA
   Director: Adrian Lyne
   Actor: Michael Douglas, Glenn Close, Anne Archer
   Script: James Dearden and Nicholas Meyer.

1. "-Well, I think I'll get saddled up and go lookin for a woman.
-Good huntin.
-Shouldn't take more than a couple of days. I'm not picky...
as long as she's smart...pretty...sweet...gentley...and tender...
and refined...lovely...carefree."

2. "-I just want to apologize to Josh's mom, and Mike's mom,
and my mom. I am so sorry! Because it was my fault. I was
the one who brought them here. I was the one that said
"keep going south." I was the one who said that we were not
lost.It was my fault, because it was my project. I am so scared!
I don't know what's out there. We are going to die out here!
I am so scared!"

3. "-Life all comes down to a few moments. This is one of them."

4. "-A relationship, I think, is like a shark. You know? It has to
constantly move forward or it dies. And I think what we got
on our hands is a dead shark."

5. "-Real diamonds! They must be worth their weight in gold!"

6. "-The son of a bitch is here. I saw him. I'm gonna get him."

ANSWER >

1. **BUTCH CASSIDY AND THE SUNDANCE KID**
   1969, USA
   Director: George Roy Hill
   Actor: Paul Newman, Robert Redford, Katharine Ross
   Script: William Goldman

2. **THE BLAIR WITCH PROJECT**
   1999, USA
   Director: Daniel Myrick, Eduardo Sánchez
   Actor: Heather Donahue, Joshua Leonard, Michael C. Williams
   Script: Daniel Myrick, Eduardo Sánchez

3. **WALL STREET**
   1987, USA
   Director: Oliver Stone
   Actor: Michael Douglas, Charlie Sheen, Daryl Hannah
   Script: Stanley Weiser and Oliver Stone.

4. **ANNIE HALL**
   1977, USA
   Director: Woody Allen
   Actor: Woody Allen, Diane Keaton, Tony Roberts
   Script: Woody Allen and Marshall Brickman.

5. **SOME LIKE IT HOT**
   1959, USA
   Director: Billy Wilder
   Actor: Jack Lemmon, Tony Curtis, Marilyn Monroe
   Script: Robert Thoeren, M. Logan, Billy Wilder and I.A.L. Diamond.

6. **THE FRENCH CONNECTION**
   1971, USA
   Director: William Friedkin
   Actor: Gene Hackman, Fernando Rey, Roy Scheider
   Script: Ernest Tidyman, Edward M. Keyes.
   Based on the book avRobin Moore.

1. "-Say Lou, didya hear the one about the guy who couldn't afford personalized plate so he went and changed his name to J3L2404? Lou: Yah, that's a good one."

2. "-You see Danny, I can deal with the bullets, and the bombs, and the blood. I don't want money, and I don't want medals. What I do want is for you to stand there in that faggoty white uniform and with your Harvard mouth extend me some fucking courtesy. You gotta ask me nicely."

3. "-What the hell you wanna go fuck around with that river for?
-Because it's there.
-It's there alright. You get in there and can't get out, you gonna wish it wasn't."

4. "-60 years old and still getting crushes on other men's wives. I hope that when I'm your age, I'll be a little bit smarter than that.
-You sure are off to a slow start."

5. "I'll feed you, I'll dress you in the morning, I'll undress you at night...I'll take care of you."

6. "-The only thing we had in common was that she was from Iowa, and I had once heard of Iowa."

ANSWER >

1. **FARGO**
    1996, USA
    Director: Joel Coen
    Actor: Frances McDormand, William H Macy, Steve Buscemi
    Script: Joel Coen and Ethan Coen.

2. **A FEW GOOD MEN**
    1992, USA
    Director: Rob Reiner
    Actor: Tom Cruise, Jack Nicholson, Demi Moore
    Script: Aaron Sorkin and Aaron Sorkin.

3. **DELIVERANCE**
    1972, USA
    Director: John Boorman
    Actor: Jon Voight, Burt Reynolds, Ned Beatty
    Script: James Dickey. Based on the book by James Dickey.

4. **NOBODY'S FOOL**
    1994, USA
    Director: Robert Benton
    Actor: Paul Newman, Jessica Tandy, Bruce Willis
    Script: Robert Benton. Based on the book by Richard Russo.

5. **NINE 1/2 WEEKS**
    1986, USA
    Director: Adrian Lyne
    Actor: Mickey Rourke, Kim Basinger, Margaret Whitton
    Script: Sarah Kernandan, Zalman King, Patricia Louisianna Knop.
    Based on the book by Elizabeth McNeill.

6. **FIELD OF DREAMS**
    1989, USA
    Director: Phil Alden Robinson
    Actor: Kevin Costner, Amy Madigan, Gaby Hoffman
    Script: Phil Alden Robinson. Based on the book W.P. Kinsella.

1. "-I don't believe that God made man in his image. 'Cause most of the shit that happens comes from man. Now I think man was made in the Devil's image. And women were created out of God. 'Cause after all, women can have babies, which is kind of like creating. And which also counts for the fact that women are so attracted to men... 'cause let's face it... the Devil is a hell of a lot more interesting! So the whole point in life is for men and women to get married... so that God and the Devil can get together and work it out."

2. "-I'll make him an offer he can't refuse."

3. "-You're a big man, but you're out of shape. With me it's a full time job. Now behave yourself. "

4. "-I'm a connoisseur of roads. I've been tasting roads my whole life. This road will never end. It probably goes all around the world."

5. "-I was murdered, an unnatural death, and now I walk the earth in limbo until the werewolf's curse is lifted."

6. "-I Should have given you to God when you were born, but I was weak and backslidin'."

ANSWER >

1. THE WITCHES OF EASTWICK
    1987, USA
    Director: George Miller
    Actor: Jack Nicholson, Cher, Susan Sarandon
    Script: Michael Cristofer. Based on the book by John Updike.

2. THE GODFATHER
    1972, USA
    Director: Francis Ford Coppola
    Actor: Marlon Brando, Al Pacino, James Caan
    Script: Mario Puzo and Francis Ford Coppola.
    Based on the book by Mario Puzo.

3. GET CARTER
    1971, UNITED KINGDOM
    Director: Mike Hodges
    Actor: Michael Caine, Ian Hendry, Britt Ekland
    Script: Mike Hodges. Based on the book by Ted Lewis (III).

4. MY OWN PRIVATE IDAHO
    1991, USA
    Director: Gus Van Sant
    Actor: River Phoenix, Keanu Reeves, James Russo
    Script: Gus Van Sant

5. AN AMERICAN WEREWOLF IN LONDON
    1981, USA
    Director: John Landis
    Actor: David Naughton, Jenny Agutter, Griffin Dunne
    Script: John Landis

6. CARRIE
    1976, USA
    Director: Brian De Palma
    Actor: Sissy Spacek, Piper Laurie, William Katt
    Script: Lawrence D. Cohen. Based on the book by Stephen King.

1. "-Don't worry! As long as you hit that wire with the connecting hook at precisely eighty-eight miles per hour the instant the lightning strikes the tower ... everything will be fine!"

2. "-They was giving me ten thousand watts a day, you know, and I'm hot to trot! The next woman takes me on's gonna light up like a pinball machine and pay off in silver dollars!"

3. "-The 70s are dead and gone. The 80s are going to be something wonderfully new and different, and so am I."

4. "-The light that burns twice as bright burns half as long and you have burned so very, very brightly, Roy."

5. "-I think you should send us the biggest transport plane you have, and take this thing to the Arctic or somewhere and drop it where it will never thaw."

6. "-Soul is the music people understand. Sure it's basic and it's simple but it's something else because it's honest, that's it. It sticks its neck out and says it straight from the heart. Sure there's a lot of different music you can get off on but soul is more than that. It grabs you by the bollocks and lifts you above the shite."

ANSWER >

1.   **BACK TO THE FUTURE**
     1985, USA
     Director: Robert Zemeckis
     Actor: Michael J Fox, Christopher Lloyd, Crispin Glover
     Script: Robert Zemeckis and Bob Gale.

2.   **ONE FLEW OVER THE CUCKOO'S NEST**
     1975, USA
     Director: Milos Forman
     Actor: Jack Nicholson, Louise Fletcher, Brad Dourif
     Script. Bo Goldman and Lawrence Hauben
     Based on the book by Ken Kesey.

3.   **CAN'T STOP THE MUSIC**
     1980, USA
     Director: Nancy Walker
     Actor: Alex Briley, David Hodo, Glenn Hughes
     Script: Alan Carr, Bronte Woodard

4.   **BLADE RUNNER**
     1982, USA
     Director: Ridley Scott
     Actor: Harrison Ford, Rutger Hauer, Sean Young
     Script: Hampton Fancher, David Webb Peoples, Roland Kibbee.
     Based on the book by Philip K. Dick.

5.   **THE BLOB**
     1958, USA
     Director:Irwin S. Yeaworth Jr.
     Actor: Steve McQueen, Aneta Corsaut, Earl Rowe
     Script: Kay Linaker, Irwing H. Millgate

6.   **THE COMMITMENTS**
     1991, UNITED KINGDOM
     Director: Alan Parker
     Actor: Robert Arkins, Michael Aherne, Angeline Ball
     Script: Dick Clement, Ian La Frenais and Roddy Doyle.
     Based on the book by Roddy Doyle.

1. "-All of you! You all killed him! And my brother, and Riff.
Not with bullets, or guns, with hate. Well now I can kill,
too, because now I have hate!"

2. "-There's nothing more irresistible to a man than a woman
who's in love with him."

3. "-For a nation of pigs, it sures seems funny that you don't eat
them! Jesus Christ forgave the bastards, but I can't! I hate!
I hate you! I hate your nation! And I hate your people!
And I fuck your sons and daughters because they're pigs!
You're all pigs!"

4. "-Geology is the study of pressure and time. Thats all it takes
really...pressure... and time... That, and big goddamn poster."

5. "-I'd say the odds against a successful escape are about 100 to
one. But may I add another word, Colonel? The odds against
survival in this camp are even worse."

6. "-Loneliness has followed me my whole life, everywhere.
In bars, in cars, sidewalks, stores, everywhere. There's
no escape. I'm God's lonely man."

ANSWER >

1. **WEST SIDE STORY**
   1961, USA
   Director: Robert Wise, Jerome Robbins
   Actor: Natalie Wood, Richard Beymer, George Chakiris
   Script: Jerome Robbins, Arthur Laurents and Ernest Lehman.
   Based on Romeo and Julia by William Shakespeare.

2. **THE SOUND OF MUSIC**
   1965, USA
   Director: Robert Wise
   Actor: Julie Andrews, Christopher Plummer, Eleanor Parker
   Script: Ernest Lehman, Richard Rodgers and Oscar Hammerstein II,
   Howard Lindsay and Russel Crouse.

3. **MIDNIGHT EXPRESS**
   1978, UNITED KINGDOM
   Director: Alan Parker
   Actor: Brad Davis, Irene Miracle, Bo Hopkins
   Script: Oliver Stone.
   Based on the book by Billy Hayes and William Hoffer.

4. **THE SHAWSHANK REDEMPTION**
   1994, USA
   Director: Frank Darabont
   Actor: Tim Robbins, Morgan Freeman, Bob Gunton
   Script: Frank Darabont. Based on the book by Stephen King.

5. **THE BRIDGE ON THE RIVER KWAI**
   1957, UNITED KINGDOM
   Director: David Lean
   Actor: William Holden, Alec Guinness, Jack Hwakins
   Script: Michael Wilson, Carl Foreman.
   Based on the book by Pierre Boulle.

6. **TAXI DRIVER**
   1976, USA
   Director: Martin Scorsese
   Actor: Robert De Niro, Cybill Shepherd, Harvey Keitel
   Script: Paul Schrader.

1. "I'm sure it comes as no great suprise to you when I say that there are little corners in everyone which were better off left alone; sicknesses, weaknesses, which-which should never be exposed. But... that's your stock in trade, isn't it - a man's weakness? And I was never really fully aware of mine... Until you brought them out."

2. "-We'll make a great team, old man. You for the words, me for the pictures. I can be your eyes."

3. "-You wanna see dry land. You really wanna see it? I'll take you there."

4. "-We must be like the ox, and have no thought, except for the Party. And have no love, but for the Angka. People starve, but we must not grow food. We must honor the comrade children, whose minds are not corrupted by the past."

5. "-It ain't so easy to shoot a man anyhow, especially if the son-of-a-bitch is shootin' back at you."

6. "-We all dream of being a child again, even the worst of us. Perhaps the worst most of all."

ANSWER >

1. **KLUTE**
   1971, USA
   Director: Alan J Pakula
   Actor: Jane Fonda, Donald Sutherland, Charles Cioffi
   Script: Andy Lewis and Dave Lewis.

2. **THE YEAR OF LIVING DANGEROUSLY**
   1983, AUSTRA
   Director: Peter Weir
   Actor: Mel Gibson, Linda Hunt, Sigourney Weaver
   Script: C.J. Kand, Peter Weir and David Williamson.
   Based on the book by C.J. Kand

3. **WATERWORLD**
   1995, USA
   Director: Kevin Reynolds
   Actor: Kevin Costner, Dennis Hopper, Jeanne Tripplehorn
   Script: Peter Rader and David Twohy.

4. **THE KILLING FIELDS**
   1984, UNITED KINGDOM
   Director: Roland Joffe
   Actor: Sam Waterston, Haing S Ngor, John Malkovich
   Script: Bruce Robinson

5. **UNFORGIVEN**
   1992, USA
   Director: Clint Eastwood
   Actor: Clint Eastwood, Gene Hackman, Morgan Freeman
   Script: David Webb Peoples.

6. **THE WILD BUNCH**
   1969, USA
   Director: Sam Peckinpah
   Actor: William Holden, Ernest Borgnine, Robert Ryan
   Script: Walon Green, Roy N. Sickner, Walon Green and
   Sam Peckinpah.

 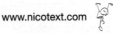

1. "-Would ya just watch the hair. Ya know, I spend a long time
    on my hair and he hit it; he hit my hair."

2. "-What do they call you?
    -Some call me one thing and others another.
    -What do they call you the most?
    -My name."

3. "-I have no plans to call on you, Clarice, the world being
    more interesting with you in it. Be sure you extend me
    the same courtesy."

4. "-I'm not going to shoot you in the state you're in.
    State of what? State of California? I know where
    the fuck I am Jack."

5. "-I'm not a fool, Plissken!
    -Call me Snake."

6. "-You've got to remember that these are just simple farmers.
    These are people of the land. The common clay of the new West.
    You know... morons."

ANSWER >

1. **SATURDAY NIGHT FEVER**
   1977, USA
   Director: John Badham
   Actor: John Travolta, Karen Lynn Gorney, Barry Miller
   Script: Nik Cohn and Norman Wexler.

2. **RED RIVER**
   1948, USA
   Director: Howard Hawks
   Actor: John Wayne, Montgomery Clift, Walter Brennan
   Script: Borden Chase, Borden Chase and Charles Schnee

3. **THE SILENCE OF THE LAMBS**
   1991, USA
   Director: Jonathan Demme
   Actor: Jodie Foster, Anthony Hopkins, Scott Glenn
   Script: Ted Tally. Based on the book by Thomas Harris.

4. **BOOGIE NIGHTS**
   1997, USA
   Director: Paul Thomas Anderson
   Actor: Mark Wahlberg, Burt Reynolds, Julianne Moore
   Script: Paul Thomas Anderson

5. **ESCAPE FROM NEW YORK**
   1981, USA
   Director: John Carpenter
   Actor: Kurt Russell, Lee Van Cleef, Ernest Borgnine
   Script: John Carpenter and Nick Castle.

6. **BLAZING SADDLES**
   1973, USA
   Director: Mel Brooks
   Actor: Cleavon Little, Gene Wilder, Harvey Korman
   Script: Andrew Bergman, Mel Brooks, Richard Pryor,
   Norman Steinberg and Alan Uger.

1. "-Nervous?
   -Yes.
   -First time?
   -No, I've been nervous lots of times."

2. "-There are ways of telling whether she is a witch.
   -Are there? Oh well, tell us!
   -Tell me. What do you do with witches?
   -Burn them!
   -And what do you burn, apart from witches?
   -More witches!
   -Wood!
   -Now, why do witches burn?
   -...because they're made of... wood?
   -Good. So how do you tell whether she is made of wood?
   -Build a bridge out of her!
   -But don't we also build bridges out of stone?
   -Oh yeah."

3. "-That's more than a dress. That's an Audrey Hepburn movie."

4. "-I tried to capture the spirit of the thing."

5. "-Up in the sky, look! It's a bird! It's a plane!"

6. "-The rest is silence."

ANSWER >

1. **AIRPLANE! / FLYING HIGH**
   1980, USA
   Director: Jim Abrahams, David Zucker, Jerry Zucker
   Actor: Robert Hays, Julie Hagerty, Robert Stack
   Script: Jim Abrahams, David Zucker and Jerry Zucker.

2. **MONTY PYTHON AND THE HOLY GRAIL**
   1974, UNITED KINGDOM
   Director: Terry Gilliam, Terry Jones
   Actor: Graham Chapman, John Cleese, Terry Gilliam
   Script: Graham Chapman, John Cleese, Eric Idle, Terry Gilliam,
   Terry Jones and Michael Palin.

3. **JERRY MAGUIRE**
   1996, USA
   Director: Cameron Crowe
   Actor: Tom Cruise, Cuba Gooding Jr, Renee Zellweger
   Script: Cameron Crowe

4. **SLAP SHOT**
   1977, USA
   Director: George Roy
   Actor: Paul Newman, Michael Ontkean, Lindsay Crouse
   Script: Nancy Dowd

5. **SUPERMAN**
   1941, USA
   Director: Dave Fleischer
   Actor: Bud Collyer (voice), Joan Alexander (voice)
   Script: Seymour Kneitel, Joe Shuster

6. **HAIR**
   1979, USA
   Director: Milos Forman
   Actor: John Savage, Treat Williams, Beverly D'Angelo
   Script: Gerome Ragni, James Rado, Galt MacDermot and
   Michael Weller.

1. "-You don't understand how i feel. I'm standing there with my pants down, and my CROTCH slung out for the world to see, and you're tellin' me that's the best you can do! Well if that's your best, then your best sucks... now i don't care what you got for selling me out but i sure as shit hope its worth it!"

2. "-Isn't that your phone number?
-Is it? I don't call myself that often"

3. "-Imagine that, seven million people all wanting to live together. New York must be the friendliest place there is."

4. "-You must have shot an awful lot of tigers Sir.
-Yes, I used a machine-gun."

5. "-The only performance that will satisfy you is when I play dead.
-Your very next role. You'll be quite convincing, I assure you."

6. "-He's just doing it to get a rise out of you. Just ignore him.
-Sweets. You couldn't ignore me if you tried. So... so.
Are you guys like boyfriend-girlfriend? Steady dates?
Lovers? Come on, sporto, level with me.
Do you slip her the hot beef injection?"

ANSWER >

1. **CITIZEN KANE**
   1941, USA
   Director: Orson Welles
   Actor: Orson Welles, Joseph Cotten, Everett Sloane
   Script: Herman J. Mankiewicz, Orson Welles and John Houseman.

2. **CHINATOWN**
   1974, USA
   Director: Roman Polanski
   Actor: Jack Nicholson, Faye Dunaway, John Huston
   Script: Robert Towne and Roman Polanski.

3. **CROCODILE DUNDEE**
   1986, AUSTRALIA
   Director: Peter Faiman
   Actor: Paul Hogan, Linda Kozlowski, John Meillon
   Script: John Cornell, Paul Hogan and Ken Shadie.

4. **THE ITALIAN JOB**
   1969, UNITED KINGDOM
   Director: Peter Collinson
   Actor: Michael Caine, Noel Coward, Maggie Blye
   Script: Troy Kennedy-Martin

5. **NORTH BY NORTHWEST**
   1959, USA
   Director: Alfred Hitchcock
   Actor: Cary Grant, Eva Marie Saint, James Mason
   Script: Ernest Lehman.

6. **THE BREAKFAST CLUB**
   1985, USA
   Director: John Hughes
   Actor: Emilio Esteves, Judd Nelson, Molly Ringwald
   Script: John Hughes

1.   "-A fellow will remember a lot of things you wouldn't think he'd remember. You take me. One day, back in 1896, I was crossing over to Jersey on the ferry, and as we pulled out, there was another ferry pulling in, and on it there was a girl waiting to get off. A white dress she had on. She was carrying a white parasol. I only saw her for one second. She didn't see me at all, but I'll bet a month hasn't gone by since that I haven't thought of that girl."

2.   "-Why don't you kiss her instead of talking her to death?
     -You want me to kiss her, Huh?
     -Ah youth is wasted on the wrong people!"

3.   "-What a fitting end to your life's pursuits. You're about to become a permanent addition to this archaeological find. Who knows? In a thousand years, even you may be worth something."

4.   "-Yippee-ki-yay, motherfucker!"

5.   "-Look speghetti arms. This is my dance Space. This is your dance space. I don't go into yours, you don't go into mine. You gotta hold the frame."

6.   "-We were all feeling a bit shagged and fagged and fashed, it being a night of no small expenditure."

ANSWER >

1. **CITIZEN KANE**
1941, USA
Director: Orson Welles
Actor: Orson Welles, Joseph Cotten, Everett Sloane
Script: Herman J. Mankiewicz, Orson Welles and John Houseman.

2. **IT'S A WONDERFUL LIFE**
1946, USA
Director: Frank Capra
Actor: James Stewart, Donna Reed, Lionel Barrymore
Script: Philip Van Doren Stern, Frances Goodrich, Albert Hackett,
Frank Capra, Jo Swerling and Michael Wilson.

3. **RAIDERS OF THE LOST ARK**
1981, USA
Director: Steven Spielberg
Actor: Harrison Ford, Karen Allen, Wolf Kahler
Script: George Lucas, Philip Kaufman and Lawrence Kasdan.

4. **DIE HARD**
1988, USA
Director: John McTiernan
Actor: Bruce Willis, Alan Rickman, Bonnie Bedelia
Script: Jeb Stuart and Steven E. de Souza.
Based on the book by Roderick Thorp.

5. **DIRTY DANCING**
1987, USA
Director: Emile Ardolino
Actor: Jennifer Grey, Patrick Swayze, Jerry Orbach
Script: Eleanor Bergstein

6. **A CLOCKWORK ORANGE**
1971, USA
Director: Stanley Kubrick
Actor: Malcolm McDowell, Patrick Magee, Adrienne Corri
Script: Stanley Kubrick. Based on the book by Anthony Burgess.

1. "-Cargo and ship destroyed. I should reach the frontier in about 6 weeks. With a little luck, the network will pick me up. This is Ripley, last survivor of The Nostromo, signing off."

2. "-Antony is dead? You say that as if it were a everyday occurence. The soup is hot, the soup is cold. Antony is alive, Antony is dead."

3. "-Well, what am I supposed to do? You won't answer my calls, you change your number. I mean, I'm not gonna be ignored, Dan!"

4. "-I don't have to take this abuse from you, I've got hundreds of people dying to abuse me."

5. "-The thing about a shark, it's got lifeless eyes, black eyes, like a doll's eyes. When it comes at you it doesn't seem to be livin'... until he bites you, and those black eyes roll over white."

6. "-How's east?
   -East?
   -Yeah, we've been going south all this time. How's east?
   -Wicked Witch of the West, Wicked Witch of the East.
   Which one was bad?
   -Wicked Witch of the West was the bad one.
   -Then we should go east."

ANSWER >

1.   ALIEN
     1979, USA
     Director: Ridley Scott
     Actor: Tom Skerritt, Sigourney Weaver, John Hurt
     Script: Dan O'Bannon, Ronald Shusett, Dan O'Bannon,
     David Giler and Walter Hill.

2.   CLEOPATRA
     1963, USA
     Director: Joseph L Mankiewicz
     Actor: Elizabeth Taylor, Richard Burton, Rex Harrison
     Script: Sidney Buchman, Ben Hecht, Ranald MacDougall and
     Joseph L. Mankiewicz. Based on the book by Carlo Mario Franzero.

3.   FATAL ATTRACTION
     1987, USA
     Director: Adrian Lyne
     Actor: Michael Douglas, Glenn Close, Anne Archer
     Script: James Dearden and Nicholas Meyer.

4.   GHOSTBUSTERS
     1984, USA
     Director: Ivan Reitman
     Actor: Bill Murray, Dan Aykroyd, Harold Ramis
     Script: Dan Aykroyd, Harold Ramis and Rick Moranis.

5.   JAWS
     1975, USA
     Director: Steven Spielberg
     Actor: Roy Scheider, Robert Shaw, Richard Dreyfuss
     Script: Peter Benchley, Carl Gottlieb, John Milius, Howard Sackler
     and Robert Shaw. Based on the book by Peter Benchley

6.   THE BLAIR WITCH PROJECT
     1999, USA
     Director: Daniel Myrick, Eduardo Sánchez
     Actor: Heather Donahue, Joshua Leonard, Michael C. Williams
     Script: Daniel Myrick, Eduardo Sánchez

1. "-Gareth used to prefer funerals to weddings; he said it was easier to get enthusiastic about a ceremony one had an outside chance of eventually being involved in."

2. "-Oh, waiter!
   -That is not a waiter, my dear, that is a butler.
   -Well, I can't yell "Oh butler!" can I? Maybe somebody's name is Butler.
   -You have a point. An idiotic one, but a point."

3. "-It's so clean out here!
   -That's because they don't throw their garbage away, they turn it into television shows."

4. "-I didn't want to do this, but I'm afraid I'm gonna have to pull rank on you. I'm with the Mattress Police. There are no tags on these mattresses."

5. "-It's like, how much more black could this be? and the answer is none. None more black."

6. "-A senatorial hearing has a way of catapulting everyone involved into the public eye with a subsequent effect on one's career. It'll be a pleasure to have you along."

ANSWER >

1. FOUR WEDDINGS AND A FUNERAL
    1994, UNITED KINGDOM
    Director: Mike Newell
    Actor: Hugh Grant, Andie MacDowell, Kristin Scott
    Script: Richard Curtis

2. ALL ABOUT EVE
    1950, USA
    Director: Joseph L Mankiewicz
    Actor: Bette Davis, Anne Baxter, George Sanders
    Script: Joseph L. Mankiewicz and Mary Orr.

3. ANNIE HALL
    1977, USA
    Director: Woody Allen
    Actor: Woody Allen, Diane Keaton, Tony Roberts
    Script: Woody Allen and Marshall Brickman.

4. FLETCH
    1985, USA
    Director: Michael Ritchie
    Actor: Chevy Chase, Dana Wheeler Nicholson, Tim Matheson
    Script: Andrew Bergman. Based on the book by Gregory McDonald.

5. THIS IS SPINAL TAP
    1984, USA
    Director: Rob Reiner
    Actor: Michael McKean, Christopher Guest, Harry Shearer
    Script: Christopher Guest, Michael McKean, Rob Reiner and
    Harry Shearer.

6. BULLITT
    1968, USA
    Director: Peter Yates
    Actor: Steve Mcqueen, Robert Vaughn, Jacqueline Bisset
    Script: Alan Trustman and Harry Kleiner.
    Based on the book by Robert L. Pike.

1. "-I know what you're thinking. Did he fire six shots or only five? Well, to tell you the truth, in all this excitement, I've kinda lost track myself. But being as this is a .44 Magnum, the most powerful handgun in the world, and would blow your head clean off, you've got to ask yourself one question: Do I feel lucky? Well, do ya punk?"

2. "-You never really understand a person until you consider things from his point of view...Until you climb inside of his skin and walk around in it."

3. "-You want answers?
-I think I'm entitled.
-You want answers?
-I want the truth!
-You can't handle the truth!"

4. "-Your eyes are full of hate, forty-one. That's good. Hate keeps a man alive."

5. "-Nobody puts baby in a coner."

ANSWER >

1.   **DIRTY HARRY**
       1971, USA
       Director: Don Siegal
       Actor: Clint Eastwood, Harry Guardino, Reni Santoni
       Script: Harry Julian Fink, Rita M. Fink, Dean Riesner and John Milius.

2.   **TO KILL A MOCKINGBIRD**
       1962, USA
       Director: Robert Mulligan
       Actor: Gregory Peck, Mary Badham, Philip Alford
       Script: Horton Foote. Based on the book by Harper Lee.

3.   **A FEW GOOD MEN**
       1992, USA
       Director: Rob Reiner
       Actor: Tom Cruise, Jack Nicholson, Demi Moore
       Script: Aaron Sorkin and Aaron Sorkin.

4.   **BEN-HUR**
       1959, USA
       Director: William Wyler
       Actor: Charlton Heston, Jack Hawkins, Stephen Boyd
       Script: Karl Tunberg, Maxwell Anderson, Christopher Fry and
       Gore Vidal. Based on the book by Lew Wallace.

5.   **DIRTY DANCING**
       1987, USA
       Director: Emile Ardolino
       Actor: Jennifer Grey, Patrick Swayze, Jerry Orbach
       Script: Eleanor Bergstein

www.nicotext.com

1. "-Don't you think I realize what's going on here, miss? Who do you think I am, huh? Don't you think I know that if I was some hotshot from out of town that pulled inside here and you guys made a reservation mistake, I'd be the first one to get a room and I'd be upstairs relaxing right now. But I'm not some hotshot from out of town, I'm a small reporter from "Rolling Stone" magazine that's in town to do an exclusive interview with Michael Jackson that's gonna be picked up by every major magazine in the country. I was gonna call the article "Michael Jackson Is Sitting On Top of the World," but now I think I might as well just call it "Michael Jackson Can Sit On Top of the World Just As Long As He Doesn't Sit in the Beverly Palm Hotel 'Cause There's No Niggers Allowed in There!""

2. "-The whole thing stinks like yesterday's diapers!"

3. "-I can't lie to you about your chances, but......
   you have my sympathies"

4. "-A heart can be broken, but it will keep beating just the same."

5. "-Come on, now. Don't be naive, Lieutenant. We both know how careers are made. Integrity is something you sell the public."

6. "-Let them hate me, so long as they fear me!"

ANSWER >

1.   **BEVERLY HILLS COP**
     1984, USA
     Director: Martin Brest
     Actor: Eddie Murphy, Judge Reinhold, John Ashton
     Script: Danilo Bach and Daniel Petrie Jr.

2.   **WHO FRAMED ROGER RABBIT**
     1988, USA
     Director: Robert Zemeckis
     Actor: Bob Hoskins, Christopher Lloyd, Joanna Cassidy
     Script: Jeffrey Price and Peter S. Seaman.
     Based on the book by Gary K. Wolf.

3.   **ALIEN**
     1979, USA
     Director: Ridley Scott
     Actor: Tom Skerritt, Sigourney Weaver, John Hurt
     Script: Dan O'Bannon, Ronald Shusett, Dan O'Bannon,
     David Giler and Walter Hill.

4.   **FRIED GREEN TOMATOES**
     1991, USA
     Director: Jon Avnet
     Actor: Kathy Bates, Jessica Tandy, Mary Stuart
     Script: Carol Sobieski, Fannie Flagg.
     Based on the book by Fannie Flagg.

5.   **BULLITT**
     1968, USA
     Director: Peter Yates
     Actor: Steve Mcqueen, Robert Vaughn, Jacqueline Bisset
     Script: Alan Trustman and Harry Kleiner.
     Based on the book by Robert L. Pike.

6.   **CALIGULA**
     1980, ITALY/USA
     Director: Tinto Brass
     Actor: Malcolm McDowell, Peter O'Toole, Teresa Ann Savoy
     Script: Gore Vidal, Bob Guccione, Giancarlo Lui, Masolino D'Amico,
     Franco Rossellini and Roberto Rossellini

www.nicotext.com

1. "-I was to extract one decagram of miolyn from four tons of earthworms.
   -Really?
   -Yes. I was on that project for five years. I was the only one who believed in it, everyone else said it couldn't be done.
   -It can't.
   -I know that now, I proved it."

2. "-Whose motorcycle is this?
   -It's a chopper, baby.
   -Whose chopper is this?
   -It's Zed's.
   -Who's Zed?
   -Zed's dead, baby. Zed's dead."

3. "-Do you have any illegal substances in the vehicle?
   -Not anymore man."

4. "-What do you all do for fun around here, listen to the grass grow?"

5. "-It's a Sicilian message.
   It means Luca Brasi sleeps with the fishes."

6. "-Every day above ground is a good day."

ANSWER >

1. **AWAKENINGS**
   1990, USA
   Director: Penny Marshall
   Actor: Robert De Niro, Robin Williams, Julie Kavner
   Script: Steven Zaillian. Based on the book by Oliver Sacks.

2. **PULP FICTION**
   1994, USA
   Director: Quentin Tarantino
   Actor: John Travolta, Samuel L Jackson, Uma Thurman
   Script: Quentin Tarantino and Roger Avary.

3. **UP IN SMOKE**
   1978, USA
   Director: Lou Adler
   Actor: Cheech Marin, Tommy Chong, Stacy Keach
   Script: Tommy Chong and Cheech Marin.

4. **BONNIE AND CLYDE**
   1967, USA
   Director: Arthur Penn
   Actor: Warren Beatty, Faye Dunaway, Michael J Pollard
   Script: David Newman (III), Robert Benton and Robert Towne.

5. **THE GODFATHER**
   1972, USA
   Director: Francis Ford Coppola
   Actor: Marlon Brando, Al Pacino, James Caan
   Script: Mario Puzo and Francis Ford Coppola.
   Based on the book by Mario Puzo.

6. **SCARFACE**
   1983, USA
   Director: Brian De Palma
   Actor: Al Pacino, Steven Bauer, Michelle Pfeiffer
   Script: Oliver Stone and Howard Hawks.
   Based on the book by Armitage Trail.

1. "-What's "forget about it"?
   -"Forget about it" is like if you agree with someone, you know,
   like "Raquel Welsh is one great piece of ass, forget about it." But
   then, if you disagree, like "A Lincoln is better than a Cadillac?
   Forget about it!" you know? But then, it's also like if something's
   the greatest thing in the world, like mingia those peppers, "forget
   about it." But it's also like saying "Go to hell!" too. Like, you know,
   like "Hey Paulie, you got a one inch pecker?" and Paulie says
   "Forget about it!" Sometimes it just means forget about it."

2. "-Have you no fear, English?
   -My fear is my concern."

3. "-I will not be threatened by a walking meat loaf!"

4. "-I know now that my wife has become host to a Candarian
   demon. I fear that the only way to stop those possessed by the
   spirits of the book is through the act of...Bodily dismemberment."

5. "-Do you know what she did, your cunting daughter?"

6. "-I just can't take no pleasure in killing. There's just some
   things you gotta do. Don't mean you have to like it."

          ANSWER >

1. **DONNIE BRASCO**
   1997, USA
   Director: Mike Newell
   Actor: Al Pacino, Johnny Depp, Michael Madsen
   Script: Paul Attanasio. Based on the book by Joseph D. Pistone and Richard Woodley.

2. **LAWRENCE OF ARABIA**
   1962, UNITED KINGDOM
   Director: David Lean
   Actor: Peter O'Toole, Alec Guinness, Anthony Quinn
   Script: T.E. Lawrence, Robert Bolt and Michael Wilson.

3. **AN AMERICAN WEREWOLF IN LONDON**
   1981, USA
   Director: John Landis
   Actor: David Naughton, Jenny Agutter, Griffin Dunne
   Script: John Landis

4. **THE EVIL DEAD**
   1983, USA
   Director: Sam Raimi
   Actor: Bruce Campbell, Ellen Sandweiss, Hal Delrich
   Script: Sam Raimi

5. **THE EXORCIST**
   1973, USA
   Director: William Friedkin
   Actor: Ellen Burstyn, Max Von Sydow, Linda Blair
   Script: William Peter Blatty

6. **THE TEXAS CHAINSAW MASSACRE**
   1974, USA
   Director: Tobe Hopper
   Actor: Marilyn Burns, Gunner Hansen, Ed Neal
   Script: Kim Henkel and Tobe Hooper.

1. "-Of course you know certain sceptics note that perhaps 10,000 of the nations's most elite highway patrolmen are out there waiting for us after we start, but let's stay positively: Think of the fact that there's not one state in the 50 that has the death penalty for speeding...although I'm not so sure about Ohio."

2. "-Look, your worshipfulness, let's get one thing straight. I take orders from just one person: Me!
-It's a wonder you're still alive."

3. "-For God's sake, Chris! The whole world is watching. We can't let him die in front of a live audience!
-He was born in front of a live audience."

4. "-I think I need a root canal. I definitely need a long, slow root canal."

5. "-Try to get this straight. There is nothing between us. There has never been anything between us. Just air."

6. "-What's your name? Come on. What's your name? Do you have a name? Do you have a police record? Where are you from?
-Disneyland."

ANSWER >

1. **THE CANNONBALL RUN**
   1981, USA
   Director: Hal Needham
   Actor: Burt Reynolds, Roger Moore, Farrah Fawcett
   Script: Brock Yates

2. **STAR WARS**
   1977, USA
   Director: George Lucas
   Actor: Mark Hamill, Harrison Ford, Carrie Fisher
   Script: George Lucas

3. **THE TRUMAN SHOW**
   1998, USA
   Director: Peter Weir
   Actor: Jim Carrey, Laura Linney, Ed Harris
   Script: Andrew Niccol.

4. **LITTLE SHOP OF HORRORS**
   1986, USA
   Director: Frank Oz
   Actor: Rick Moranis, Ellen Greene, Vincent Gardenia
   Script: Charles B. Griffith and Howard Ashman.

5. **SINGIN' IN THE RAIN**
   1952, USA
   Director: Gene Kelly, Stanley Donen
   Actor: Gene Kelly, Debbie Reynolds, Donald O'Conner
   Script: Betty Comden and Adolph Green.

6. **THE HITCHER**
   1986, USA
   Director: Robert Harmon
   Actor: Rutger Hauer, C Thomas Howell, Jennifer Jason Leigh
   Script: Eric Red

1. "-Now there's only two reasons why you didnt sit on that step next to me. Either you too scared boy or you just hate niggers. What is it boy, you too scared?
-Naahh, I just hate niggers."

2. "-Some birds aren't meant to be caged. Their feathers are just too bright."

3. "-Listen, why don't we begin with what happened tonight, hmm? Perhaps you could...you know, give me some of the details.
-I was here, Doc..,died, you came.
-That's it?
-I'm a demon for details."

4. "-Keaton once said, "I don't believe in God, but I'm afraid of him." Well I believe in God, and the only thing that scares me is Keyser Soze."

5. "-Why don't you knock it off with them negative waves? Why don't you dig how beautiful it is out here? Why don't you say something righteous and hopeful for a change?"

6. "-Time marches on and sooner or later you realize it is marchin' across your face."

ANSWER >

1.   ESCAPE FROM ALCATRAZ
      1979, USA
      Director: Donald Siegel
      Actor: Clint Eastwood, Patrick McGoohan, Roberts Blossom
      Script: Richard Tuggle. Based on the book by J. Campbell Bruce.

2.   THE SHAWSHANK REDEMPTION
      1994, USA
      Director: Frank Darabont
      Actor: Tim Robbins, Morgan Freeman, Bob Gunton
      Script: Frank Darabont. Based on the book by Stephen King.

3.   MARATHON MAN
      1976, USA
      Director: John Schlesinger
      Actor: Dustin Hoffman, Laurence Olivier, Roy Scheider
      Script: Robert Towne and William Goldman.
      Based on the book by William Goldman.

4.   THE USUAL SUSPECTS
      1995, USA
      Director: Bryan Singer
      Actor: Stephen Baldwin, Gabriel Byrne, Chazz PalMinteri
      Script: Christopher McQuarrie.

5.   KELLY'S HEROES
      1970, USA
      Director: Brian G Hutton
      Actor: Clint Eastwood, Telly Savalas, Don Rickles
      Script: Troy Kennedy-Martin

6.   STEEL MAGNOLIAS
      1989, USA
      Director: Herbert Ross
      Actor: Sally Field, Dolly Parton, Julia Roberts
      Script: Robert Harling.

1. "-I'm a star. I'm a fucking star"

2. "-You gonna kill me now, Snake?
   -I'm too tired. Maybe later"

3. "-Who's that there?
   -I don't know... Must be a king...
   -Why?
   -He hasn't got shit all over him."

4. "-You know where you're going?
   -Uptown, I believe?
   -Uptown? You headed into Harlem!
   -Well you just stay on the tail of that jukebox and there's
   an extra twenty dollars in it for you.
   -Hey man, for twenty bucks I'd take you to a Ku Klux Klan
   cookout!"

5. "-Now comes the part where I relieve you, the little people, of
   the burden of your failed and useless lives. But remember, as
   my plastic surgeon always said: if you gotta go, go with a smile."

6. "-You guys got nothing to worry about, I'm a professional.
   -A professional what?"

ANSWER >

1.   **BOOGIE NIGHTS**
      1997, USA
      Director: Paul Thomas Anderson
      Actor: Mark Wahlberg, Burt Reynolds, Julianne Moore
      Script: Paul Thomas Anderson

2.   **ESCAPE FROM NEW YORK**
      1981, USA
      Director: John Carpenter
      Actor: Kurt Russell, Lee Van Cleef, Ernest Borgnine
      Script: John Carpenter and Nick Castle.

3.   **MONTY PYTHON AND THE HOLY GRAIL**
      1974, UNITED KINGDOM
      Director: Terry Gilliam, Terry Jones
      Actor: Graham Chapman, John Cleese, Terry Gilliam
      Script: Graham Chapman, John Cleese, Eric Idle, Terry Gilliam,
      Terry Jones and Michael Palin.

4.   **LIVE AND LET DIE,**
      1973, UNITED KINGDOM
      Director: Guy Hamilton
      Actor: Roger Moore, Yaphet Kotto, Jane Seymour
      Script: Tom Mankiewicz. Based on the book by Ian Fleming.

5.   **BATMAN**
      1989, USA
      Director: Tim Burton
      Actor: Jack Nicholson, Michael Keaton, Kim Basinger
      Script: Bob Kane, Sam Hamm and Warren Skaaren.

6.   **FERRIS BUELLER'S DAY OFF**
      1986, USA
      Director: John Hughes
      Actor: Matthew Broderick, Alan Ruck, Mia Sara
      Script: John Hughes

1. "-You wanta go for a ride?
   -No thanks.
   -No thanks. What does that mean?
   -I don't want to go.
   -Go where?
   -On a ride.
   -A ride? Hell, that's a good idea. Okay, let's go. Hey, let's go."

2. "-A drug person can learn to cope with seeing their dead
   grandmother crawling up their leg with a knife in her teeth...
   But no one should be asked to handle this trip."

3. "-Hollis seems to think you're an innocent man.
   -Well, I've been accused of a lot of things before,
   Mrs. Mulwray, but never that."

4. "You were only supposed to blow the bloody doors off."

5. "-You are not machines! You are men! With the love of humanity
   in your hearts! Don't hate! Only the unloved hate; the unloved and
   the unnatural. Soldiers!"

6. "-Hey, hey, hey, baby. What do you say?
   -Don't say anything and we'll get along just fine."

ANSWER >

1.   **BLUE VELVET**
1986, USA
Director: David Lynch
Actor: Kyle MacLachlan, Isabella Rossellini, Dennis Hopper
Script: David Lynch

2.   **FEAR AND LOATHING IN LAS VEGAS**
1998, USA
Director: Terry Gilliam
Actor: Johnny Depp, Benicio Del Toro, Tobey Maguire
Script: Terry Gilliam, Tony Grisoni, Tod Davies and Alex Cox.
Based on the book by Hunter S. Thompson.

3.   **CHINATOWN**
1974, USA
Director: Roman Polanski
Actor: Jack Nicholson, Faye Dunaway, John Huston
Script: Robert Towne and Roman Polanski.

4.   **THE ITALIAN JOB**
1969, UNITED KINGDOM
Director: Peter Collinson
Actor: Michael Caine, Noel Coward, Maggie Blye
Script: Troy Kennedy-Martin

5.   **THE GREAT DICTATOR**
1940, USA
Director: Charles Chaplin
Actor: Charles Chaplin, Jack Oakie, Reginald Gardiner
Script: Charles Chaplin

6.   **AMERICAN GRAFFITI**
1973, USA
Director: George Lucas
Actor: Richard Dreyfuss, Ronny Howard, Paul LeMat
Script: George Lucas, Gloria Katz and Willard Huyck.

1. "-Even a poisonous snake isn't bad. You just have to keep away from the sharp end."

2. "-Luke, you can destroy the Emperor. He has foreseen this. Join me and together we will rule the galaxy as father and son!"

3. "-You don't understand. I coulda had class. I coulda been a contender. I coulda been somebody, instead of a bum, which is what I am, let's face it. It was you, Charley."

4. "-I was married for four years, and pretended to be happy; and I had six years of analysis, and pretended to be sane. My husband ran off with his boyfriend, and I had an affair with my analyst, who told me I was the worst lay he'd ever had."

5. "-I think voting is the opium of the masses in this country. Every four years you deaden the pain."

6. "-Now hold it, hold it. We're about to accuse Haldeman, who only happens to be the second most important man in this country, of conducting a criminal conspiracy from inside the White House. It would be nice if we were right."

ANSWER >

1. **THE GODS MUST BE CRAZY**
1980, BOTSWANA
Director: Jamie Uys
Actor: Marius Weyers, Sandra Prinsloo, N!xau
Script: Jamie Uys

2. **THE EMPIRE STRIKES BACK**
1980, USA
Director: Irwin Kershner
Actor: Mark Hamill, Harrison Ford, Carrie Fisher
Script: George Lucas, Leigh Brackett and Lawrence Kasdan.

3. **WATERFRONT**
1950 UNITED KINGDOM
Director: Michael Anderson
Actor: Robert Newton, Kathleen Harrison
Script: John Brophy, Paul Soskin

4. **NETWORK**
1976, USA
Director: Sidney Lumet
Actor: William Holden, Faye Dunaway, Peter Finch
Script: Paddy Chayefsky

5. **REDS**
1981, USA
Director: Warren Beatty
Actor: Warren Beatty, Diane Keaton, Edward Herrmann
Script: Warren Beatty, Trevor Griffiths, Elaine May, John Reed (II),
Jeremy Pikser and Peter S. Feibleman.

6. **ALL THE PRESIDENTS MEN**
1976, USA
Director: Alan J Pakula
Actor: Robert Redford, Dustin Hoffman, Jason Roberts
Script: William Goldman.
Based on the book by Carl Bernstein and Bob Woodward.

1. "-A good fight should be like a small play but, played seriously. When the opponent expands, I contract. When he contracts, I expand. And when the opportunity presents itself, I do not hit! It hits all by itself."

2. "-Who are these men?
   -They're associated with Special Forces.
   -What? What does that mean?
   -It means that they are associated with Special Forces."

3. "-Were not students, were The Ramones."

4. "-Oh, the Indian is hot. I go for exotic types, especially when they're half-naked.
   -Lulu!
   -You tell him I'll make up for all the indignities they suffered in "Roots."."

5. "-Don't take that tone with me young man. I fought the war for your sort.
   -I bet you're sorry you won."

6. "-Well, I've always believed that if done properly, armed robbery doesn't have to be an unpleasant experience."

ANSWER >

1.   ENTER THE DRAGON
      1973, USA
      Director: Robert Clouse
      Actor: Bruce Lee, John Saxon, Jim Kelly
      Script: Michael Allin

2.   NO WAY OUT
      1987, USA
      Director: Roger Donaldson
      Actor: Kevin Costner, Gene Hackman, Sean Young
      Script: Robert Garland. Based on the book by Kenneth Fearing.

3.   ROCK 'N' ROLL HIGH SCHOOL
      1979, USA
      Director: Allan Arkush, Joe Dante
      Actor: P.J Soles, Vincent van Patten, Clint Howard
      Script: Richard Whitley, Russ Dronch

4.   CAN'T STOP THE MUSIC
      1980, USA
      Director: Nancy Walker
      Actor: Alex Briley, David Hodo, Glenn Hughes
      Script: Alan Carr, Bronte Woodard

5.   A HARD DAY'S NIGHT
      1964, UNITED KINGDOM
      Director: Richard Lester
      Actor: John Lennon, Paul McCartney, George Harrison
      Script: Alun Owen

6.   THELMA & LOUISE
      1991, USA
      Director: Ridley Scott
      Actor: Susan Sarandon, Geena Davis, Harvey Keitel
      Script: Callie Khouri.

1. "-I am awake.
    -Your eyes are shut.
    -Who you gonna believe?"

2. "-But what is so alarming about laughter?
    -Laughter kills fear, and without fear there can be no faith,
    because without fear of the Devil there is no more need of God."

3. "-When you love someone, you've gotta trust them. There's
    no other way. You've got to give them the key to everything
    that's yours. Otherwise, what's the point? And, for a while,
    I believed that's the kind of love I had."

4. "-He's a man from outer space and we're taking him
    to his spaceship.
    -Well, can't he just beam up?
    -This is REALITY, Greg."

5. "-Like the sign says, "speed's just a question of money.
    How fast can you go?"

6. "-I should have killed myself when he took me. After the first
    time, before we were married, Ralph promised never again.
    He promised me and I believed him. But sin never dies.
    Sin never dies."

                              ANSWER >

1. MILLER'S CROSSING
    1990, USA
    Director: Joel Coen
    Actor: Gabriel Byrne, Albert Finney, Marcia Gay Harden
    Script: Joel Coen and Ethan Coen.
    Based on the book by Dashiell Hammett.

2. THE NAME OF THE ROSE
    1986, FRANCE/ITALY/WEST-GERMANY
    Director: Jean Jacques Annaud
    Actor: Sean Connery, F Murray Abraham, Christian Slater
    Script: Andrew Birkin, Gérard Brach, Howard Franklin and
    Alain Godard. Based on the book by Umberto Eco.

3. CASINO
    1995, USA
    Director: Martin Scorsese
    Actor: Robert De Niro, Sharon Stone Joe Pesci
    Script: Nicholas Pileggi and Martin Scorsese.
    Based on the book by Nicholas Pileggi.

4.

    E.T THE EXTRA-TERRESTRIAL
    1982, USA
    Director: Steven Spielberg
    Actor: Dee Wallace, Henry Thomas, Peter Coyote
    Script: Melissa Mathison

5. MAD MAX
    1979, AUSTRALIEN
    Director: George Miller
    Actor: Mel Gibson, Joanne Samuel, Hugh Keays Byrne
    Script: James McCausland and George Miller.

6. CARRIE
    1976, USA
    Director: Brian De Palma
    Actor: Sissy Spacek, Piper Laurie, William Katt
    Script: Lawrence D. Cohen. Based on the book by Stephen King.

1. "-Is there something bad here?
   -Well, you know, Doc, when something happens, you can leave
   a trace of itself behind. Say like, if someone burns toast. Well,
   maybe things that happen leave other kinds of traces behind.
   Not things that anyone can notice, but things that people who
   "shine" can see."

2. "-You've got to believe me, Officer, he is coming to Haddonfield...
   Because I know him - I'm his doctor! You must be ready for him...
   If you don't, it's your funeral!"

3. "-Queen Elizabeth is a man! Prince Charles is a pervert!
   Winston Churchill was full of shit! Shakespeare's French!"

4. "-Why are you laughing?
   -Your going to rent cars?!
   -That's right, I know a lot about cars. I've been stealing
   them since I was 14."

5. "-Keep talking Matty, experience has shown that I can be
   convinced of anything."

6. "-There are watchers in this world and there are doers.
   And the watchers sit around watching the doers do.
   Tonight you watched, and I did."

ANSWER >

1. **THE SHINING**
   1980, USA
   Director: Stanley Kubrick
   Actor: Jack Nicholson, Shelley Duvall, Danny Lloyd
   Script: Stanley Kubrick and Diane Johnson.
   Based on the book by Stephen King.

2. **HALLOWEEN**
   1978, USA
   Director: John Carpenter
   Actor: Donald Pleasence, Jamie Lee Curtis, Nancy Loomis
   Script: John Carpenter and Debra Hill.

3. **AN AMERICAN WEREWOLF IN LONDON**
   1981, USA
   Director: John Landis
   Actor: David Naughton, Jenny Agutter, Griffin Dunne
   Script: John Landis

4. **CARLITO'S WAY**
   1993, USA
   Director: Brian De Palma
   Actor: Al Pacino, Sean Penn, Penelope Ann Miller
   Script: David Koepp. Based on the book by Edwin Torres.

5. **BODY HEAT**
   1981, USA
   Director: Lawrence Kasdan
   Actor: William Hurt, Kathleen Turner, Richard Crenna
   Script: Lawrence Kasdan

6. **BAREFOOT IN THE PARK**
   1967, USA
   Director: Gene Saks
   Actor: Robert Redford, Jane Fonda, Charles Boyer
   Script: Neil Simon

1. "-Speed is like a dozen transatlantic flights without ever getting off the plane. Time change. You lose, you gain. Makes no difference so long as you keep taking the pills. But sooner or later you've got to get out because it's crashing, and then all at once the frozen hours melt out through the nervous system and seep out the pores."

2. "-Normally, both of you would be dead as fucking fried chicken by now, but since I'm in a transitional period, I don't want to kill either one of your asses."

3. "-Most people don't know how they're gonna feel from one moment to the next. But a dope fiend has a pretty good idea. All you gotta do is look at the labels on the little bottles."

4. "-He's pissed at YOU, Wirf.
   -Only because he knows I won't go away.
   -I know how he feels."

5. "-This is your life and it's ending one minute at a time."

6. "-Do you just want to lose weight, or are you looking to increase strength and flexibility as well?
   -I want to look good naked!"

ANSWER >

1. **WITHNAIL AND I**
   1986, UNITED KINGDOM
   Director: Bruce Robinson
   Actor: Richard E Grant, Paul McGann, Richard Griffiths
   Script: Bruce Robinson.

2. **PULP FICTION**
   1994, USA
   Director: Quentin Tarantino
   Actor: John Travolta, Samuel L Jackson, Uma Thurman
   Script: Quentin Tarantino and Roger Avary.

3. **DRUGSTORE COWBOY**
   1989, USA
   Director: Gus Van Sant
   Actor: Matt Dillon, Kelly Lynch, James Remar
   Script: Gus Van Sant, Daniel Yost and William S. Burroughs.
   Based on the book by James Fogle..

4. **NOBODY'S FOOL**
   1994, USA
   Director: Robert Benton
   Actor: Paul Newman, Jessica Tandy, Bruce Willis
   Script: Robert Benton. Based on the book by Richard Russo.

5. **FIGHT CLUB**
   1999, USA
   Director: David Fincher
   Actor: Brad Pitt, Edward Norton, Helena Bonham Carter
   Script: Jim Uhls. Based on the book by Chuck Palahniuk.

6. **AMERICAN BEAUTY**
   1999, USA
   Director: Sam Mendes
   Actor: Kevin Spacey, Annette Bening, Thora Birch
   Script: Alan Ball

1. "-Hawkeye Pierce? I got a twix from headquarters about you...says you stole a jeep.
   -No sir, no, I didn't steal it. No, it's right outside."

2. "-I would suggest that those of us with stout hearts and trim waistlines start using the stairs.
   -That's 135 floors.
   -All downhill."

3. "-I saw a young officer on deck the other day, and he looked DAMN familiar... even with his clothes on!
   -So... he recognized ya, so?
   -So doesn't that bother you?
   -If it bothered me, I wouldn'ta married ya.
   -Well first you arrested me six times!
   -Well I had to figure out some way to keep you off the streets... until you'd marry me!"

4. "-I'm loud, darling, but never cheap."

5. "-At birth, I was cast into a flaming pit of scum forgotten by God."

6. "-Neighbors bring food with death, and flowers with sickness, and little things in between."

ANSWER >

1. **MASH**
   1970, USA
   Director: Robert Altman
   Actor: Donald Sutherland, Elliott Gould, Tom Skerritt
   Script: Ring Lardner Jr.
   Based on the book by Richard Hooker.

2. **THE TOWERING INFERNO**
   1974, USA
   Director: John Guillermin, Irwin Allen
   Actor: Steve Mcqueen, Paul Newman, William Holden
   Script: Stirling Silliphant. Based on the book by Richard Martin Stern,
   Thomas N. Scortia and Frank M. Robinson.

3. **THE POSEIDON ADVENTURE**
   1972, USA
   Director: Ronald Neame
   Actor: Gene Hackman, Ernest Borgnine, Red Buttons
   Script: Wendell Mayes and Stirling Silliphant.
   Based on the book by Paul Gallico.

4. **THE CRYING GAME**
   1992, UNITED KINGDOM
   Director: Neil Jordan
   Actor: Stephan Rea, Miranda Richardson, Forest Whitaker
   Script: Neil Jordan

5. **NATURAL BORN KILLERS**
   1994, USA
   Director: Oliver Stone
   Actor: Woody Harrelson, Juliette Lewis, Robert Downey Jr
   Script: Quentin Tarantino, David Veloz, Richard Rutowski and
   Oliver Stone.

6. **TO KILL A MOCKINGBIRD**
   1962, USA
   Director: Robert Mulligan
   Actor: Gregory Peck, Mary Badham, Philip Alford
   Script: Horton Foote. Based on the book by Harper Lee.

1. "-You know, we are sitting here like a couple of regular fellows and if I have to go out there and put you down, I'll tell you, I won't like it. But if it's between you and some poor bastard whose wife you're gonna turn into a widow, buddy, you are going down.
-There is a flip side to this coin. What if you do get me boxed in and I will have to put you down? Cause no matter what, you will not get in my way. We've been face to face, yeah. But I will not hesitate, not for a second."

2. "-We split the car.
-How the fuck do you split a car, you dummy? With a fucking chainsaw?"

3. "-I'm a marked man in this department. For what?
-I've already arranged a transfer for you.
-To where? China?"

4. "Go ahead, punk, make my day."

5. "-Water polo, isn't that dangerous?
-It sure is. I had two ponies drowned under me."

6. "-The mirror...it's broken
-Yes, I know. I like it that way. Makes me look the way I feel."

ANSWER >

1.   **HEAT**
       1995, USA
       Director: Michael Mann
       Actor: Al Pacino, Robert De Niro, Val Kilmer
       Script: Michael Mann

2.   **FARGO**
       1996, USA
       Director: Joel Coen
       Actor: Frances McDormand, William H Macy, Steve Buscemi
       Script: Joel Coen and Ethan Coen.

3.   **SERPICO**
       1973, USA
       Director: Sidney Lumet
       Actor: Al Pacino, John Randolph, Jack Kehoe
       Script: Waldo Salt and Norman Wexler.
       Based on the book by Peter Maas.

4.   **DIRTY HARRY**
       1971, USA
       Director: Don Siegal
       Actor: Clint Eastwood, Harry Guardino, Reni Santoni
       Script: Harry Julian Fink, Rita M. Fink, Dean Riesner and John Milius.

5.   **SOME LIKE IT HOT**
       1959, USA
       Director: Billy Wilder
       Actor: Jack Lemmon, Tony Curtis, Marilyn Monroe
       Script: Robert Thoeren, M. Logan, Billy Wilder and I.A.L. Diamond.

6.   **THE APARTMENT**
       1960, USA
       Director: Billy Wilder
       Actor: Jack Lemmon, Shirley MacLaine, Fred MacMurray
       Script: Billy Wilder and I.A.L. Diamond.

1. "-Ehm, look. Sorry, sorry. I just, ehm, well, this is a very stupid question and..., particularly in view of our recent shopping excursion, but I just wondered, by any chance, ehm, eh, I mean obviously not because I guess I've only slept with 9 people, but-but I-I just wondered... ehh. I really feel, ehh, in short, to recap it slightly in a clearer version, eh, the words of David Cassidy in fact, eh, while he was still with the Partridge family, eh, "I think I love you," and eh, I-I just wondered by any chance you wouldn't like to...Eh... Eh... No, no, no of course not... I'm an idiot, he's not... Excellent, excellent, fantastic, eh, I was gonna say lovely to see you, sorry to disturb... Better get on...
-That was very romantic.
-Well, I thought it over a lot, you know, I wanted to get it just right."

2. "-I love you more than any woman's ever loved a rabbit."

3. "-They drew first blood, not me. They drew first blood."

4. "-She's wonderful! Where did you find her?
-976-BABE."

5. "-Now I have a machine gun. Ho ho ho."

6. "-I don't mind a reasonable amount of trouble."

ANSWER >

1.   FOUR WEDDINGS AND A FUNERAL
     1994, UNITED KINGDOM
     Director: Mike Newell
     Actor: Hugh Grant, Andie MacDowell, Kristin Scott
     Script: Richard Curtis

2.   WHO FRAMED ROGER RABBIT
     1988, USA
     Director: Robert Zemeckis
     Actor: Bob Hoskins, Christopher Lloyd, Joanna Cassidy
     Script: Jeffrey Price and Peter S. Seaman.
     Based on the book by Gary K. Wolf.

3.   FIRST BLOOD
     1982, USA
     Director: Ted Kotcheff
     Actor: Sylvester Stallone, Richard Crenna, Brian Dennehy
     Script: Michael Kozoll, William Sackheim, Sylvester Stallone.
     Based on the book by David Morrell.

4.   PRETTY WOMAN
     1990, USA
     Director: Garry Marshall
     Actor: Richard Gere, Julia Roberts, Ralph Bellamy
     Script: J.F Lawton

5.   DIE HARD
     1988, USA
     Director: John McTiernan
     Actor: Bruce Willis, Alan Rickman, Bonnie Bedelia
     Script: Jeb Stuart and Steven E. de Souza.
     Based on the book by Roderick Thorp.

6.   THE MALTESE FALCON
     1941, USA
     Director: John Huston
     Actor: Humphrey Bogart, Mary Astor, Peter Lorre
     Script: John Huston. Based on the book by Dashiell Hammett.

1. "-Hey look, mister, we serve hard drinks in here for men who want to get drunk fast and we don't need any characters around to give the joint atmosphere. Is that clear or do I have to slip you my left for a convincer?"

2. "-Where were you last night?
-That's so long ago, I don't remember.
-Will I see you tonight?
-I never make plans that far ahead."

3. "-Can you imagine the life he must have had?
-Yes, I believe I can.
-No, I don't believe so. I don't think any of us can."

4. "-Doesn't it hurt?
-Well, I sort of lay there in pain, but I love it. I really love it. I lay there hovering between consciousness and unconsciousness. It's really the greatest."

5. "-Are you suicidal?
-Only in the mornings."

6. "-Oh no, you can't take my photograph.
-Oh, I'm sorry, you believe it will take your spirit away?
-No, you got the lens-cap on."

ANSWER >

1.   IT'S A WONDERFUL LIFE
      1946, USA
      Director: Frank Capra
      Actor: James Stewart, Donna Reed, Lionel Barrymore
      Script: Philip Van Doren Stern, Frances Goodrich, Albert Hackett,
      Frank Capra, Jo Swerling and Michael Wilson.

2.   CASABLANCA
      1942, USA
      Director: Michael Curtiz
      Actor: Humphrey Bogart, Ingrid Bergman, Paul Henreid
      Script: Murray Burnett, Joan Alison, Julius J. Epstein, Philip G.
      Epstein, Howard K and, Casey Robinson.

3.   THE ELEPHANT MAN
      1980, USA
      Director: David Lynch
      Actor: Anthony Hopkins, John Hurt, Anne Bancroft
      Script: Christopher De Vore, Eric Bergren and David Lynch.
      Based on the book by Sir Frederick Treves and Ashley Montagu.

4.   LOLITA,
      1962, UNITED KINGDOM
      Director: Stanley Kubrick
      Actor: James Mason, Shelley Winters, Peter Sellers
      Script: Vladimir Nabokov and Stanley Kubrick
      Based on the book by Vladimir Nabokov.

5.   OCEAN'S ELEVEN
      1960, USA
      Director: Lewis Milestone
      Actor: Frank Sinatra, Dean Martin, Sammy Davis Jr
      Script: George Clayton Johnson, Jack Golden Russell,
      Harry Brown, Charles Lederer and Billy Wilder.

6.   CROCODILE DUNDEE
      1986, AUSTRALIA
      Director: Peter Faiman
      Actor: Paul Hogan, Linda Kozlowski, John Meillon
      Script: John Cornell, Paul Hogan and Ken Shadie.

www.nicotext.com

1. "-We had two bags of grass, seventy-five pellets of mescaline, five sheets of high powered blotter acid, a salt shaker half full of cocaine and a whole galaxy of multicolored uppers, downers, screamers, leaughers...Also a quart of tequilla, a quart of rum, a case of budweiser, a pint of raw ether, and two dozen amyls. But the only thing that worried me was the ehter. There is nothing in the world more helpless and irresponsible than a man in the depths of an ether binge... And i knew we'd get into that rotten stuff pretty soon."

2. "-You know something, Verna, if I turn my back for long enough for Big Ed to put a hole in it, there'd be a hole in it."

3. "-God is not on our side because he hates idiots also."

4. "Life moves pretty fast. If you don't stop and look around once in a while, you could miss it."

5. "-You know, you guys are amazing. You think not getting caught in a lie is the same thing as telling the truth!"

6. "-Saayyy, nice beaver.
-Thanks. I just had it stuffed."

ANSWER >

1. **FEAR AND LOATHING IN LAS VEGAS**
1998, USA
Director: Terry Gilliam
Actor: Johnny Depp, Benicio Del Toro, Tobey Maguire
Script: Terry Gilliam, Tony Grisoni, Tod Davies and Alex Cox.
Based on the book by Hunter S. Thompson.

2. **WHITE HEAT**
1949, USA
Director: Raoul Walsh
Actor: James Cagney, Virginia Mayo, Edmond O'Brien
Script: Virginia Kellogg, Ivan Goff and Ben Roberts.

3. **A FISTFULL OF DOLLARS**
1964, ITALY
Director: Sergio Leone
Actor: Clint Eastwood, Marianne Kand, Gian maria Volonté
Script: A. Bonzzoni, Victor Andrés Catena

4. **FERRIS BUELLER'S DAY OFF**
1986, USA
Director: John Hughes
Actor: Matthew Broderick, Alan Ruck, Mia Sara
Script: John Hughes

5. **THREE DAYS OF THE CONDOR**
1975, USA
Director: Sydney Pollack
Actor: Robert Redford, Faye Dunaway, Cliff Robertson
Script: Lorenzo Semple Jr and David Rayfiel.
Based on the book by James Grady.

6. **THE NAKED GUN:**
FROM THE FILES OF POLICE SQUAD
1988, USA
Director: David Zucker
Actor: Leslie Nielsen, George Kennedy, Priscilla Presley
Script: Jim Abrahams, David Zucker and Pat Proft.

1. "-I think now, looking back, we did not fight the enemy, we fought ourselves. The enemy was in us. The war is over for me now, but it will always be there, the rest of my days. As I'm sure Elias will be, fighting with Barnes for what Rhah called "possession of my soul." There are times since, I've felt like a child, born of those two fathers. But be that as it may, those of us who did make it have an obligation to build again. To teach to others what we know, and to try with what's left of our lives to find a goodness and a meaning to this life."

2. "-Alright. I'll do it. I'will show you how a Prussian officer fights.
    -And I will show you where the Iron Crosses grow."

3. "-The greatest trick the devil ever pulled was convincing the world he didn't exist."

4. "-You make me sick with your heroics. There's a stench of death about you. You carry it in your pack like the plague."

5. "-My mother told me to never do this."

6. "-She just goes a little mad sometimes. We all go a little mad sometimes. Haven't you?"

ANSWER >

1.   PLATOON
        1986, USA
        Director: Oliver Stone
        Actor: Tom Berenger, Willem Dafoe, Charlie Sheen
        Script: Oliver Stone

2.   CROSS OF IRON
        1977, UNITED KINGDOM/WESTGERMANY
        Director: Sam Peckinpah
        Actor: James Coburn, Maximilian Schell, James Mason
        Script: Julius J. Epstein, James Hamilton and Walter Kelley.
        Based on the book by Frederick Forsyth.

3.   THE USUAL SUSPECTS
        1995, USA
        Director: Bryan Singer
        Actor: Stephen Baldwin, Gabriel Byrne, Chazz PalMinteri
        Script: Christopher McQuarrie.

4.   THE BRIDGE ON THE RIVER KWAI
        1957, UNITED KINGDOM
        Director: David Lean
        Actor: William Holden, Alec Guinness, Jack Hwakins
        Script: Michael Wilson, Carl Foreman.
        Based on the book by Pierre Boulle.

5.   THE HITCHER
        1986, USA
        Director: Robert Harmon
        Actor: Rutger Hauer, C Thomas Howell, Jennifer Jason Leigh
        Script: Eric Red

6.   PSYCHO
        1960, USA
        Director: Alfred Hitchcook
        Actor: Anthony Perkins, Janet Leigh, Vera Miles
        Script: Joseph Stefano.
        Based on the book by Robert Bland.

1. "-I only have sex with a guy for money.
    -Yeah, I know.
    -And two guys can't love each other.
    -Yeah. Well, I don't know. I mean....I mean for me, I could love
    someone even if I, you know, wasn't paid for it. I love you
    and....you don't pay me."

2. "-And maybe there's no peace in this world, for us or for anyone
    else, I don't know. But I do know that, as long as we live, we
    must remain true to ourselves."

3. "-You wanna know how you do it? Here's how, they pull a knife,
    you pull a gun. He sends one of yours to the hospital, you send
    on of his to the morgue! That's the Chicago way, and that's how
    you get Capone! Now do you want to do that? Are you ready to
    do that?"

4. "-You'll live with the stink of the streets all your life.
    -I like the stink of the streets. It cleans out my lungs.
    And it gives me a hard-on."

5. "-You don't make up for your sins in church. You do it in the
    streets. You do it at home. The rest is bullshit and you know it."

6. "-A favor will kill you faster than a bullet."

ANSWER >

1. **MY OWN PRIVATE IDAHO**
   1991, USA
   Director: Gus Van Sant
   Actor: River Phoenix, Keanu Reeves, James Russo
   Script: Gus Van Sant

2. **SPARTACUS**
   1960, USA
   Director: Stanley Kubrick
   Actor: Kirk Douglas, Laurence Olivier, Jean Simmons
   Script: Dalton Trumbo, Calder Willingham and Peter Ustinov.
   Based on the book by Howard Fast.

3. **THE UNTOUCHABLES**
   1987, USA
   Director: Brian De Palma
   Actor: Kevin Costner, Sean Connery, Charles Martin Smith
   Script: David Mamet. Based on the book by Oscar Fraley and Eliot
   Ness and Paul Robsky.

4. **ONCE UPON A TIME IN AMERICA**
   1984, USA
   Director: Sergio Leone
   Actor: Robert De Niro, James Woods, Elizabeth McGovern
   Script: Leonardo Benvenuti, Piero De Bernardi, Enrico Medioli,
   Franco Arcalli, Franco Ferrini, Sergio Leone, Stuart Kaminsky and
   Ernesto Gastaldi. Based on the book by Harry Grey.

5. **MEAN STREETS**
   1973, USA
   Director: Martin Scorsese
   Actor: Robert De Niro, Harvey Keitel, David Proval
   Script: Martin Scorsese and Mardik Martin.

6. **CARLITO'S WAY**
   1993, USA
   Director: Brian De Palma
   Actor: Al Pacino, Sean Penn, Penelope Ann Miller
   Script: David Koepp. Based on the book by Edwin Torres.

1. "-What if I were to call the police and tell them there's a bloke staying in me hotel that's planning to shoot somebody?
   -You wouldn't do that
   .-Why not?
   -Because I know you wear purple underwear.
   -And what's that supposed to mean?
   -Think about it."

2. "-I know it was you Fredo. You broke my heart. You broke my heart. You broke my heart."

3. "-What's your last name?
   -Same as my mother's and father's.
   -And what's that?
   -Which one, my mother's or my father's?
   -Either!
   -The same as mine!"

4. "-I always like a little pussy after lunch."

5. "-Did you lose your mind all at once, or was it a slow, gradual process?"

ANSWER >

1. **GET CARTER**
   1971, UNITED KINGDOM
   Director: Mike Hodges
   Actor: Michael Caine, Ian Hendry, Britt Ekland
   Script: Mike Hodges. Based on the book by Ted Lewis.

2. **THE GODFATHER PART II**
   1974, USA
   Director: Francis Ford Coppola
   Actor: Al Pacino, Robert De Niro, Robert Duvall,
   Script: Mario Puzo and Francis Ford Coppola.

3. **XANADU**
   1980, USA
   Director: Robert Greenwald
   Actor: Olivia Newton John, Gene Kelly, Michael Beck
   Script: Richard Christian Danus and Marc Reid Rubel.

4. **THE WITCHES OF EASTWICK**
   1987, USA
   Director: George Miller
   Actor: Jack Nicholson, Cher, Susan Sarandon
   Script: Michael Cristofer. Based on the book by John Updike.

5. **THE FISHER KING**
   1991, USA
   Director: Terry Gilliam
   Actor: Robin Williams, Jeff Bridges, Amanda Plummer
   Script: Richard LaGravenese

1. "-Nobody's been seen coming in or out for 3 years.
   Except every morning there are 9 empty cans of tuna fish
   sitting outside the door.
   -Who do you suppose lives there?
   -Sounds like a big cat with a can opener."

2. "-Picture the best orgasm you ever had. Multiply it by
   a thousand and you're still nowhere near it."

3. "-You're a very strange person, Robert. I mean, what would it
   come to? If a person has no love for himself, no respect for him
   self, no love of his friends, family, work, something
   -how can he ask for love in return? I mean, why should he ask
   for it?"

4. "-I wonder how such a degenerated person ever reached a
   position of authority in the Army Medical Corps!
   -He was drafted."

5. "-Miriam! I have to take your blood pressure!
   -I've been sitting still for 25 years. You missed your chance."

6. "-A woman has her feelings.
   -But Dil, you're not a woman!
   -Details , baby! Details!"

ANSWER >

1. **BAREFOOT IN THE PARK**
   1967, USA
   Director: Gene Saks
   Actor: Robert Redford, Jane Fonda, Charles Boyer
   Script: Neil Simon

2. **TRAINSPOTTING**
   1996, UNITED KINGDOM
   Director: Danny Boyle
   Actor: Ewan McGregor, Ewan Bremmer, Jonny Lee Miller
   Script: John Hodge. Based on the book by Irvine Welsh.

3. **FIVE EASY PIECES**
   1970, USA
   Director: Bob Rafelson
   Actor: Jack Nicholson, Karen Black, Billy Green
   Script: Carole Eastman and Bob Rafelson.

4. **MASH**
   1970, USA
   Director: Robert Altman
   Actor: Donald Sutherland, Elliott Gould, Tom Skerritt
   Script: Ring Lardner Jr. Based on the book by Richard Hooker.

5. **AWAKENINGS**
   1990, USA
   Director: Penny Marshall
   Actor: Robert De Niro, Robin Williams, Julie Kavner
   Script: Steven Zaillian. Based on the book by Oliver Sacks.

6. **THE CRYING GAME**
   1992, UNITED KINGDOM
   Director: Neil Jordan
   Actor: Stephan Rea, Miranda Richardson, Forest Whitaker
   Script: Neil Jordan

1. "-Once upon a time, a woman was picking up firewood. She came upon a poisonous snake frozen in the snow. She took the snake home and nursed it back to health. One day the snake bit her on the cheek. As she lay dying, she asked the snake, "Why have you done this to me?" And the snake answered, "Look, bitch, you knew I was a snake."."

2. "-Frank, let's face it. Who can trust a cop who don't take money?"

3. "-I come from a musical family.
   -My father was a famous conductor
   -Where did your father conduct?
   -On the Baltimore & Ohio."

4. "-I used to live like Robinson and Crusoe, shipwrecked among 8 million people but one day I saw a footprint in the sand and there you were."

5. "-There comes a time that a piano realizes that it has not written a concerto."

6. "-The point is, ladies and gentlemen, that greed, for lack of a better word, is good. Greed is right. Greed works."

ANSWER >

1. **NATURAL BORN KILLERS**
   1994, USA
   Director: Oliver Stone
   Actor: Woody Harrelson, Juliette Lewis, Robert Downey Jr
   Script: Quentin Tarantino, David Veloz, Richard Rutowski and
   Oliver Stone.

2. **SERPICO**
   1973, USA
   Director: Sidney Lumet
   Actor: Al Pacino, John Randolph, Jack Kehoe
   Script: Waldo Salt and Norman Wexler.
   Based on the book by Peter Maas.

3. **SOME LIKE IT HOT**
   1959, USA
   Director: Billy Wilder
   Actor: Jack Lemmon, Tony Curtis, Marilyn Monroe
   Script: Robert Thoeren, M. Logan, Billy Wilder and I.A.L. Diamond.

4. **THE APARTMENT**
   1960, USA
   Director: Billy Wilder
   Actor: Jack Lemmon, Shirley MacLaine, Fred MacMurray
   Script: Billy Wilder and I.A.L. Diamond.

5. **ALL ABOUT EVE**
   1950, USA
   Director: Joseph L Mankiewicz
   Actor: Bette Davis, Anne Baxter, George Sanders
   Script: Joseph L. Mankiewicz and Mary Orr.

6. **WALL STREET**
   1987, USA
   Director: Oliver Stone
   Actor: Michael Douglas, Charlie Sheen, Daryl Hannah
   Script: Stanley Weiser and Oliver Stone.

 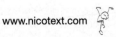

1. "-Class isn't something you buy. Look at you, you've got on a 500-dollar suit and you're still a low-life.
-Yeah, but I look good."

2. "-Then you jump first.
-No, I said.
-What's the matter with you?
-I can't swim.
-Why you crazy, the fall will probably kill you."

3. "-Try to imagine all life as you know it stopping instantaneously and every molecule in your body exploding at the speed of light."

4. "-What we were after now was the old surprise visit. That was a real kick and good for laughs and lashings of the old ultraviolence."

5. "-He's got a client who shot his wife in the head six times. Six times, can you imagine it? I mean, even twice would be overdoing it, don't you think?"

6. "-We're more likely to believe a respected local businessman than some foul-mouth jerk from out of town.
-Foul-Mouth? Fuck you man."

1.   48HRS
        1982, USA
        Director: Walter Hill
        Actor: Nick Nolte, Eddie Murphy, Annette O'Toole
        Script: Roger Spottiswoode, Walter Hill, Larry Gross, Steven E. de
        Souza and Jeb Stuart.

2.   BUTCH CASSIDY AND THE SUNDANCE KID
        1969, USA
        Director: George Roy Hill
        Actor: Paul Newman, Robert Redford, Katharine Ross
        Script: William Goldman

3.   GHOSTBUSTERS
        1984, USA
        Director: Ivan Reitman
        Actor: Bill Murray, Dan Aykroyd, Harold Ramis
        Script: Dan Aykroyd, Harold Ramis and Rick Moranis.

4.   A CLOCKWORK ORANGE
        1971, USA
        Director: Stanley Kubrick
        Actor: Malcolm McDowell, Patrick Magee, Adrienne Corri
        Script: Stanley Kubrick. Based on the book by Anthony Burgess.

5.   THE BIRDS
        1963, USA
        Director: Alfred Hitchcock
        Actor: Rod Taylor, Tippi Hedren, Jessica Tandy
        Script: Daphne Du Maurier and Evan Hunter.

6.   BEVERLY HILLS COP
        1984, USA
        Director: Martin Brest
        Actor: Eddie Murphy, Judge Reinhold, John Ashton
        Script: Danilo Bach and Daniel Petrie Jr.

1. "-Back there I could fly a gunship, I could drive a tank, I was in charge of million dollar equipment. Back here I can't even hold a job washin cars."

2. "-How odd that it should end this way for us after so many stimulating encounters. I almost regret it. Where shall I find a new adversary so close to my own level?
   -Try the local sewer."

3. "-If you were not a bride I would kiss you goodbye.
   -If I were not a bride, there would be no goodbyes to be said."

4. "-I still wish you had't done that, Hildy.
   -Done What?
   -Divorced me. It makes a man feel he's not Wanted."

5. "-Send me postcards from exotic ports of call...isn't that what you call them? Exotic ports of call?
   -YOU'RE exotic!"

6. "-Man who catch fly with chopstick accomplish anything.
   -Ever catch one?
   -Not yet."

ANSWER >

1. **FIRST BLOOD**
   1982, USA
   Director: Ted Kotcheff
   Actor: Sylvester Stallone, Richard Crenna, Brian Dennehy
   Script: Michael Kozoll, William Sackheim, Sylvester Stallone.
   Based on the book by David Morrell.

2. **RAIDERS OF THE LOST ARK**
   1981, USA
   Director: Steven Spielberg
   Actor: Harrison Ford, Karen Allen, Wolf Kahler
   Script: George Lucas, Philip Kaufman and Lawrence Kasdan.

3. **BEN-HUR**
   1959, USA
   Director: William Wyler
   Actor: Charlton Heston, Jack Hawkins, Stephen Boyd
   Script: Karl Tunberg, Maxwell Anderson, Christopher Fry and
   Gore Vidal. Based on the book by Lew Wallace.

4. **HIS GIRL FRIDAY**
   1940, USA
   Director: Howard Hawks
   Actor: Cary Grant, Rosalind Russell, Ralph Bellamy
   Script: Ben Hecht, Charles MacArthur and Charles Lederer.

5. **NO WAY OUT**
   1987, USA
   Director: Roger Donaldson
   Actor: Kevin Costner, Gene Hackman, Sean Young
   Script: Robert Garland. Based on the book by Kenneth Fearing.

6. **THE KARATE KID**
   1984, USA
   Director: John G Avildsen
   Actor: Ralph Macchio, Noriyuki Morita, Elisabeth Shue
   Script: Robert Mark Kamen

1. "-Excuse me, what is your name? I'm Bob Woodward,
   of the Washington Post.
   -Markham.
   -Markham. Mr. Markham, are you here in connection with
   the Watergate burglary?
   -I'm not here."

2. "-If I die, I'm sorry for all the bad things I did to you. And if I
   live, I'm sorry for all the bad things I'm gonna do to you."

3. "-Well obviously those three girls were just the wrong three girls."

4. "-What do you play?
   -I used to play football in school.
   -I mean what instrument.
   -I don't.
   -Then what are you doing here?
   -Well, I saw everyone else lining up so I thought
   you were selling drugs."

5. "-And crawling on this planet's face, some insects called the
   human race. Lost in time. And lost in space... and meaning."

6. "-Cosmo, call me a cab.
   -OK, you're a cab."

ANSWER >

1. **ALL THE PRESIDENTS MEN**
   1976, USA
   Director: Alan J Pakula
   Actor: Robert Redford, Dustin Hoffman, Jason Roberts
   Script: William Goldman.
   Based on the book by Carl Bernstein and Bob Woodward.

2. **ALL THAT JAZZ**
   1979, USA
   Director: Bob Fosse
   Actor: Roy Schneider, Jessica Lange, Ann Reinking
   Script: Robert Alan Aurthur and Bob Fosse.

3. **CABARET**
   1972, USA
   Director: Bob Fosse
   Actor: Liza Minelli, Michael York, Helmut Griem
   Script: John Van Druten, Joe Masteroff, Jay Presson Allen and
   Hugh Wheeler. Based on the book by Christopher Isherwood.

4. **THE COMMITMENTS**
   1991, UNITED KINGDOM
   Director: Alan Parker
   Actor: Robert Arkins, Michael Aherne, Angeline Ball
   Script: Dick Clement, Ian La Frenais and Roddy Doyle.
   Based on the book by Roddy Doyle.

5. **THE ROCKY HORROR PICTURE SHOW**
   1975, USA
   Director: Jim Sharman
   Actor: Tim Curry, Susan Sarandon, Barry Bostwick
   Script: Richard O'Brien, Jim Sharman

6. **SINGIN' IN THE RAIN**
   1952, USA
   Director: Gene Kelly, Stanley Donen
   Actor: Gene Kelly, Debbie Reynolds, Donald O'Conner
   Script: Betty Comden and Adolph Green.

1. "Survival kit contents check. In them you'll find: one .45 caliber automatic; two boxes of ammunition; four days concentrated emergency raisons; one drug issue containing: antibiotics, morphine, vitamin pills, pep pills, sleeping pills, tranquilizer pills; one miniature combination Russian phrase book and bible; one hundred dollars in rubles; one hundred dollars in gold; nine packs of chewing gum; one issue of prophylactics; three lipsticks; three pair a nylon stockings. Shoot, a fellah could have a pretty good weekend in Vegas with all that stuff."

2. "-It looks like you will see Berlin before I do."

3. "-Don't feel bad about losing your virtue. I sort of knew you would. Everybody always does."

4. "-Have you any famous last words?
   -Not yet.
   -Not yet? Is that famous?"

5. "-Do you believe in God, Sergeant?
   -I believe God is a sadist, but probably doesn't even know it."

6. "-You forgive me?
   -Nothing is forgiven. Nothing."

ANSWER >

1. DR STRANGELOVE OR: HOW I LEARNED TO STOP
    WORRYING AND LOVE THE BOMB
    1963, UNITED KINGDOM
    Director: Stanley Kubrick
    Actor: Peter Sellers, George C Scott, Sterling Hayden
    Script: Stanley Kubrick, Terry Southern and Peter George III.
    Based on the book by Peter George.

2. THE GREAT ESCAPE
    1962, USA
    Director: John Sturges,
    Actor: Steve McQueen, James Garner, Richard Attenborough
    Script: James Clavell and W.R. Burnett.
    Based on the book by Paul Brickhill.

3. KLUTE
    1971, USA
    Director: Alan J Pakula
    Actor: Jane Fonda, Donald Sutherland, Charles Cioffi
    Script: Andy Lewis and Dave Lewis.

4. THE ADVENTURES OF BARON MUNCHAUSEN
    1989, UNITED KINGDOM
    Director: Terry Gilliam
    Actor: John Neville, Eric Idle, Sarah Polley
    Script: Terry Gilliam and Charles McKeown.
    Based on the book avv Rudolph Erich Raspe.

5. CROSS OF IRON
    1977, UNITED KINGDOM/WEST-GERMANY
    Director: Sam Peckinpah
    Actor: James Coburn, Maximilian Schell, James Mason
    Script: Julius J. Epstein, James Hamilton and Walter Kelley.
    Based on the book by Frederick Forsyth.

6. THE KILLING FIELDS
    1984, UNITED KINGDOM
    Director: Roland Joffe
    Actor: Sam Waterston, Haing S Ngor, John Malkovich
    Script: Bruce Robinson

1. "-Somewhere out there is the beast and he's hungry tonight.
   -Have you ever gotten into a mistake that you just can't
   get out of?
   -There is a way out of everything, man. Just keep your
   pecker hard and your powder dry and the world will turn."

2. "-The army doesn't like more than one disaster in a day.
   -Looks bad in the newspapers and upsets civilians
   at their breakfast."

3. "-I've killed women and children. I've killed everything that walks
   or crawls at one time or another. And I'm here to kill you, Little Bill,
   for what you done to Ned."

4. "-What I like and what I need are two different things."

5. "-Four dollars? You know what four dollars buys today?
   It don't even buy three dollars!"

6. "-Have you read the Bible, Pete?
   -Holy Bible?
   -Yeah.
   -Yeah, I think so. Anyway, I've heard about it."

ANSWER >

1. **PLATOON**
   1963, USA
   Director: Oliver Stone
   Actor: Tom Berenger, Willem Dafoe, Charlie Sheen
   Script: Oliver Stone

2. **ZULU**
   1963, UNITED KINGDOM
   Director: Cy Endfield
   Actor: Stanley Baker, Jack Hawkins, Ulla Jacobsson
   Script: John Prebble, John Prebble and Cy Endfield.

3. **UNFORGIVEN**
   1992, USA
   Director: Clint Eastwood
   Actor: Clint Eastwood, Gene Hackman, Morgan Freeman
   Script: David Webb Peoples.

4. **THE WILD BUNCH**
   1969, USA
   Director: Sam Peckinpah
   Actor: William Holden, Ernest Borgnine, Robert Ryan
   Script: Walon Green, Roy N. Sickner, Walon Green and
   Sam Peckinpah.

5. **SATURDAY NIGHT FEVER**
   1977, USA
   Director: John Badham
   Actor: John Travolta, Karen Lynn Gorney, Barry Miller
   Script: Nik Cohn and Norman Wexler.

6. **BARTON FINK**
   1991, USA
   Director: Joel Coen
   Actor: John Turturro, John Goodman, Judy Davis
   Script: Ethan Coen and Joel Coen.

1. "-Money is the world's curse.
    -May the Lord smite me with it! And may I never recover!"

2. "-Then one day I hear "Reach for it mister!" I spun around,
    and there I was standing face to face with a six year old kid.
    Well, I just laid down my guns and walked away. Little bastard
    shot me in the ass!"

3. "-You got a letter from headquarters this morning.
    -What is it?
    -It's a big building where generals meet, but that's not important."

4. "-We are the Knights who say... NI!"

5. "-You know, I got a hunch, fat man. I got a hunch that it's me
    from here on in. One ball, corner pocket. I mean, that ever happen
    to you? You know, all of a sudden you feel like you just can't
    miss? 'Cause I dreamed about this game, fat man. I dreamed
    about it every night on the road. Five ball. You know, this is my
    table, man. I own it."

6. "-What do you want?
    -Oh, little song, little dance, Batman's head on a lance..."

ANSWER >

1. FIDDLER ON THE ROOF
    1971, USA
    Director: Norman Jewison
    Actor: Topol, Norma Crane, Leonard Frey
    Script: Joseph Stein. Based on the book by Sholom Aleichem.

2. BLAZING SADDLES
    1973, USA
    Director: Mel Brooks
    Actor: Cleavon Little, Gene Wilder, Harvey Korman
    Script: Andrew Bergman, Mel Brooks, Richard Pryor,
    Norman Steinberg and Alan Uger.

3. AIRPLANE! / FLYING HIGH
    1980, USA
    Director: Jim Abrahams, David Zucker, Jerry Zucker
    Actor: Robert Hays, Julie Hagerty, Robert Stack
    Script: Jim Abrahams, David Zucker and Jerry Zucker.

4. MONTY PYTHON AND THE HOLY GRAIL
    1974, UNITED KINGDOM
    Director: Terry Gilliam, Terry Jones
    Actor: Graham Chapman, John Cleese, Terry Gilliam
    Script: Graham Chapman, John Cleese, Eric Idle, Terry Gilliam,
    Terry Jones and Michael Palin.

5. THE HUSTLER
    1961, USA
    Director: Robert Rossen
    Actor: Paul Newman, Jackie Gleason, Piper Lauire
    Script: Sidney Carroll and Robert Rossen.
    Based on the book by Walter Tevis.

6. BATMAN
    1989, USA
    Director: Tim Burton
    Actor: Jack Nicholson, Michael Keaton, Kim Basinger
    Script: Bob Kane, Sam Hamm and Warren Skaaren.

1. "-Your middle name is Ralph, as in puke, your birthdate's March 12th, you're 5'9 and a half, you weigh 130 pounds and your social security number is 049380913.
-Wow! Are you psychic?
-No.
-Well, would you mind telling me how you know all this about me?
-I stole your wallet."

2. "-If you were happy every day of your life you wouldn't be a human being. You'd be a game-show host."

3. "-I'll send you a love letter! Straight from my heart, fucker! You know what a love letter is? It's a bullet from a fucking gun, fucker! You recieve a love letter from me, you're fucked forever! You understand, fuck? I'll send you straight to hell, fucker!"

4. "-A copper, a copper, how do you like that boys? A copper and his name is Fallon. And we went for it, I went for it. Treated him like a kid brother. And I was gonna split fifty-fifty with a copper!"

5. "-I hope he likes spagetti, they serve it four times a day in Italian prisons!"

6. "-Your car's uglier than I am...That didn't come out right."

ANSWER >

1.   THE BREAKFAST CLUB
       1985, USA
       Director: John Hughes
       Actor: Emilio Esteves, Judd Nelson, Molly Ringwald
       Script: John Hughes

2.   HEATHERS
       1989, USA
       Director: Michael Lehmann
       Actor: Winona Ryder, Christian Slater, Shannen
       Doherty Script: Daniel Waters

3.   BLUE VELVET
       1986, USA
       Director: David Lynch
       Actor: Kyle MacLachlan, Isabella Rossellini, Dennis Hopper
       Script: David Lynch

4.   WHITE HEAT
       1949, USA
       Director: Raoul Walsh
       Actor: James Cagney, Virginia Mayo, Edmond O'Brien
       Script: Virginia Kellogg, Ivan Goff and Ben Roberts.

5.   THE ITALIAN JOB
       1969, UNITED KINGDOM
       Director: Peter Collinson
       Actor: Michael Caine, Noel Coward, Maggie Blye
       Script: Troy Kennedy-Martin

6.   AMERICAN GRAFFITI
       1973, USA
       Director: George Lucas
       Actor: Richard Dreyfuss, Ronny Howard, Paul LeMat
       Script: George Lucas, Gloria Katz and Willard Huyck.

1. "-Is drinking a way of killing yourself?
   -Or, is killing myself a way of drinking?"

2. "-All I know is that this violates every canon of respectable
   broadcasting. We're not a respectable network. We're a
   whorehouse network, and we have to take whatever we can get."

3. "-Hey, you wanna hear my philosophy of life? Do it to him
   before he does it to you."

4. "-Our knowledge as made us cynical; our cleverness, hard
   and unkind. We think too much and feel too little."

5. "-I'm gonna buy me a herd of chorus girls and make
   'em dance on my bed."

6. "-This may seem like a really stupid question...
   -There *are* no stupid questions.
   -You inherit 5 million dollars the same day aliens land on the
   earth and say they're going to blow it up in 2 days.
   What do you do?
   -That's the stupidest question I've ever heard."

ANSWER >

1.   **LEAVING LAS VEGAS**
     1995, USA
     Director: Mike Figgis
     Actor: Nicolas Cage, Elisabeth Shue, Julian Sands
     Script: Mike Figgis. Based on the book by John O'Brien.

2.   **NETWORK**
     1976, USA
     Director: Sidney Lumet
     Actor: William Holden, Faye Dunaway, Peter Finch
     Script: Paddy Chayefsky

3.   **WATERFRONT**
     1950 UNITED KINGDOM
     Director: Michael Anderson
     Actor: Robert Newton, Kathleen Harrison
     Script: John Brophy, Paul Soskin

4.   **THE GREAT DICTATOR**
     1940, USA
     Director: Charles Chaplin
     Actor: Charles Chaplin, Jack Oakie, Reginald Gardiner
     Script: Charles Chaplin

5.   **JAILHOUSE ROCK**
     1957, USA
     Director: Richard Thorpe
     Actor: Elvis Presley, Judy Tyler, Vaughn Taylor
     Script: Nedrick Young and Guy Trosper.

6.   **HEATHERS**
     1989, USA
     Director: Michael Lehmann
     Actor: Winona Ryder, Christian Slater, Shannen Doherty
     Script: Daniel Waters

1. "-They wanted in Hollywood to make the definitive spy picture. And they came to me to supervise the project, you know, because I think that, if you know me at all, you know that death is my bread and danger my butter - oh, no, danger's my bread, and death is my butter. No, no, wait. Danger's my bread, death no, death is - no, I'm sorry. Death is my - death and danger are my various breads and various butters."

2. "I don't remember yesterday. Today it rained."

3. "-Muhammad Ali, he was like a sleeping elephant. You can do whatever you want around a sleeping elephant; whatever you want. But when he wakes up, he tramples everything."

4. "-Don't cry at the begining of a date. Cry at the end, like I do."

5. "-He says the sun came out last night. He says it sang to him."

6. "-Ay, fight and you may die, run and you'll live. At least a while. And dying in your beds many years from now, would you be willing to trade all the days from this day to that for one chance, just one chance to come back here and tell our enemies that they may take our lives, but they'll never take our freedom?"

ANSWER >

1. **WHAT'S UP TIGER LILY?**
   1966, JAPAN
   Director: Senkichi Taniguchi
   Actor: Tatsuya Mihashi, Miya Hana, Eiko Wakabayashi
   Script: Woody Allen, Julie Bennett, Frank Buxton, Louise Lasser,
   Len Maxwell, Mickey Rose and Bryan Wilson.

2. **THREE DAYS OF THE CONDOR**
   1975, USA
   Director: Sydney Pollack
   Actor: Robert Redford, Faye Dunaway, Cliff Robertson
   Script: Lorenzo Semple Jr and David Rayfiel.
   Based on the book by James Grady.

3. **WHEN WE WERE KINGS**
   1996, USA
   Director: Leon Gast
   Actor: Muhammad Ali, George Forman, Don King

4. **JERRY MAGUIRE**
   USA
   Director: Cameron Crowe
   Actor: Tom Cruise, Cuba Gooding Jr, Renee Zellweger
   Script: Cameron Crowe

5. **CLOSE ENCOUNTERS OF THE THIRD KIND**
   1977, USA
   Director: Steven Spielberg
   Actor: Richard Dreyfuss, Francois Truffaut, Teri Garr
   Script: Steven Spielberg, Hal Barwood, Jerry Belson, John Hill and
   Matthew Robbins.

6. **BRAVEHEART**
   1995, USA
   Director: Mel Gibson
   Actor: Mel Gibson, Sophie Marceau, Patrick McGoohan
   Script: Randall Wallace

1. "-I don't feel the sickness yet, but it's in the post. That's for sure. I'm in the junkie limbo at the moment. Too ill to sleep. Too tired to stay awake, but the sickness is on its way. Sweat, chills, nausea. Pain and craving. A need like nothing else I've ever known will soon take hold of me. It's on its way."

2. "-Even a stopped clock tells the right time twice a day, and for once I'm inclined to believe Withnail is right. We are indeed drifting into the arena of the unwell."

3. "-May I please see your license?
   -Huh?
   -Your license, may I please see your license?
   -Hey man, ain't it up there on the bumper man?"

4. "-He who draws the sword from the stone, he shall be king. Arthur, you're the one!"

5. "-How did you know? How did you know I'd respond to you the way I have?
   -I saw myself in you."

6. "-If anything in this life is certain, if history has taught us anything, it is that you can kill anyone."

ANSWER >

1. **TRAINSPOTTING**
   1996, UNITED KINGDOM
   Director: Danny Boyle
   Actor: Ewan McGregor, Ewan Bremmer, Jonny Lee Miller
   Script: John Hodge. Based on the book by Irvine Welsh.

2. **WITHNAIL AND I**
   1986, UNITED KINGDOM
   Director: Bruce Robinson
   Actor: Richard E Grant, Paul McGann, Richard Griffiths
   Script: Bruce Robinson

3. **UP IN SMOKE**
   1978, USA
   Director: Lou Adler
   Actor: Cheech Marin, Tommy Chong, Stacy Keach
   Script: Tommy Chong and Cheech Marin.

4. **EXCALIBUR**
   1981, UNITED KINGDOM
   Director: John Boorman
   Actor: Nicol Williamson, Nigel Terry, Helen Mirren
   Script: Rospo Pallenberg and John Boorman.
   Based on the book by Thomas Malory.

5. **NINE 1/2 WEEKS**
   1986, USA
   Director: Adrian Lyne
   Actor: Mickey Rourke, Kim Basinger, Margaret Whitton
   Script: Sarah Kernandan, Zalman King, Patricia Louisianna Knop.
   Based on the book by Elizabeth McNeill.

6. **THE GODFATHER PART II**
   1974, USA
   Director: Francis Ford Coppola
   Actor: Al Pacino, Robert De Niro, Robert Duvall,
   Script: Mario Puzo and Francis Ford Coppola.

1. "-You know, we always called each other goodfellas. Like, you'd say to somebody: "You're gonna like this guy; he's all right. He's a goodfella. He's one of us." You understand? We were goodfellas, wiseguys."

2. "-You see, I have a story too, Mr. Bailey. I had a friend once. A dear friend. I turned him in to save his life. He died. But he wanted it that way. Things went bad for my friend, and they went bad for me too."

3. "-You wanna fuck with me? Okay. You wanna play rough? Okay, Say hello to my little friend."

4. "-Are you afraid to die, Spartacus?
   -No more than I was to be born."

5. "-Well, Denham, the airplanes got him.
   -Oh no, it wasn't the airplanes. It was beauty that killed the beast."

6. "-Ray, people will come Ray. They'll come to Iowa for reasons they can't even fathom. They'll turn up your driveway not knowing for sure why they're doing it. They'll arrive at your door as innocent as children, longing for the past."

ANSWER >

1. **GOODFELLAS**
   1990, USA
   Director: Martin Scorsese
   Actor: Robert De Niro, Ray Liotta, Joe Pesci
   Script: Nicholas Pileggi and Martin Scorsese.
   Based on the book by Nicholas Pileggi.

2. **ONCE UPON A TIME IN AMERICA**
   1984, USA
   Director: Sergio Leone
   Actor: Robert De Niro, James Woods, Elizabeth McGovern
   Script: Leonardo Benvenuti, Piero De Bernardi, Enrico Medioli,
   Franco Arcalli, Franco Ferrini, Sergio Leone, Stuart Kaminsky and
   Ernesto Gastaldi. Based on the book by Harry Grey.

3. **SCARFACE**
   1983, USA
   Director: Brian De Palma
   Actor: Al Pacino, Steven Bauer, Michelle Pfeiffer
   Script: Oliver Stone and Howard Hawks. Based on the book by
   Armitage Trail.

4. **SPARTACUS**
   1960, USA
   Director: Stanley Kubrick
   Actor: Kirk Douglas, Laurence Olivier, Jean Simmons
   Script: Dalton Trumbo, Calder Willingham and Peter Ustinov.
   Based on the book by Howard Fast.

5. **KING KONG**
   1976, USA
   Director: John Guillermin
   Actor: Jeff Bridges, Charles Grodin, Jessica Lange
   Script: Merian C. Cooper, Edgar Wallace, James Ashmore Creelman,
   Ruth Rose and Lorenzo Semple Jr.

6. **FIELD OF DREAMS**
   1989, USA
   Director: Phil Alden Robinson
   Actor: Kevin Costner, Amy Madigan, Gaby Hoffman
   Script: Phil Alden Robinson. Based on the book W.P. Kinsella.

1. "-I hope they don't hang you, precious, by that sweet neck. The chances are you'll get off with life. That means if you're a good girl, you'll be out in 20 years. I'll be waiting for you. If they hang you...I'll always remember you."

2. "-Inside the Ark are treasures beyond your wildest aspirations. You want to see it opened as well as I. Indiana, we are simply passing through history. This, this "is" history."

3. "-I'm tired, I've been drinking since nine o'clock, my wife is vomiting, there's been a lot of screaming going on around here!"

4. "-We were attracted to each other at the party, that was obvious! You're on your own for the night, that's also obvious... We're two adults."

5. "-This was no boat accident. It was no boat propeller, it wasn't any coral reef, and it wasn't Jack the Ripper. It was a shark."

6. "-DO YOU SEE THE LIGHT?!!
-What light?!
-DO YOU SEEEE THE LIGHT?!
-YES!! YES!! JESUS H. TAP-DANCING CHRIST...I HAVE SEEN THE LIGHT!!!"

ANSWER >

1. THE MALTESE FALCON
    1941, USA
    Director: John Huston
    Actor: Humphrey Bogart, Mary Astor, Peter Lorre
    Script: John Huston. Based on the book by Dashiell Hammett.

2. RAIDERS OF THE LOST ARK
    1981, USA
    Director: Steven Spielberg
    Actor: Harrison Ford, Karen Allen, Wolf Kahler
    Script: George Lucas, Philip Kaufman and Lawrence Kasdan.

3. WHO'S AFRAID OF VIRGINIA WOOLF
    1966, USA
    Director: Mike Nichols
    Actor: Elizabeth Taylor, Richard Burton, George Segal
    Script: Edward Albee and Ernest Lehman.

4. FATAL ATTRACTION
    1987, USA
    Director: Adrian Lyne
    Actor: Michael Douglas, Glenn Close, Anne Archer
    Script: James Dearden and Nicholas Meyer.

5. JAWS
    1975, USA
    Director: Steven Spielberg
    Actor: Roy Scheider, Robert Shaw, Richard Dreyfuss
    Script: Peter Benchley, Carl Gottlieb, John Milius, Howard Sackler
    and Robert Shaw. Based on the book by Peter Benchley

6. THE BLUES BROTHERS
    1980, USA
    Director: John Landis
    Actor: John Belushi, Dan Aykroyd, Cap Calloway
    Script: Dan Aykroyd and John Landis.

1. "-You see a girl a couple of times a week and sooner or later she thinks you'll divorce your wife. Not fair, is it?
-No, especially to your wife."

2. "-Crucifixion?
-Yes.
-Good. Out of the door, line on the left, one cross each.
-Crucifixion?
-Er, no, freedom actually.
-What?
-Yeah, they said I hadn't done anything and I could go and live on an island somewhere.
-Oh I say, that's very nice. Well, off you go then.
-No, I'm just pulling your leg, it's crucifixion really.
-Oh yes, very good. Well...
-Yes I know, out of the door, one cross each, line on the left."

3. "-You see, Mr. Scott? In the water I'm a very skinny lady!"

4. "-You know those days when you get the mean reds?"

5. "-Flowers are simply tarts; prostitutes for the bees."

6. "-Where ya from man?
-Hard to say."

ANSWER >

1.   **THE APARTMENT**
     1960, USA
     Director: Billy Wilder
     Actor: Jack Lemmon, Shirley MacLaine, Fred MacMurray
     Script: Billy Wilder and I.A.L. Diamond.

2.   **MONTY PYTHON'S LIFE OF BRIAN**
     1979, UNITED KINGDOM
     Director: Terry Jones
     Actor: Graham Chapman, John Cleese, Terry Gilliam
     Script: Graham Chapman, John Cleese, Terry Gilliam, Eric Idle,
     Terry Jones and Michael Palin.

3.   **THE POSEIDON ADVENTURE**
     1972, USA
     Director: Ronald Neame
     Actor: Gene Hackman, Ernest Borgnine, Red Buttons
     Script: Wendell Mayes and Stirling Silliphant.
     Based on the book by Paul Gallico.

4.   **BREAKFAST AT TIFFANY'S**
     1961, USA
     Director: Blake Edwards
     Actor: Audrey Hepburn, George Peppard
     Script: Truman Capote, George Axelrod

5.   **WITHNAIL AND I**
     1986, UNITED KINGDOM
     Director: Bruce Robinson
     Actor: Richard E Grant, Paul McGann, Richard Griffiths
     Script: Bruce Robinson

6.   **EASY RIDER**
     1969, USA
     Director: Dennis Hopper
     Actor: Peter Fonda, Dennis Hopper, Jack Nicholson
     Script: Peter Fonda, Dennis Hopper and Terry Southern.

1. "-Jesus, Bob, you never told us anything about not mentioning dogs.
-The reason nobody mentioned dogs, Rick, is that to mention the dog would have been a hex in itself.
-All right, well, now we are on the subject, are there an other stupid things we aren't supposed to mention that will affect our future?"

2. "-Lower your flags and march straight back to England, stopping at every home to beg forgiveness for a hundred years of theft, rape, and murder. Do this and your men shall live. Do it not, and every one of you will die today."

3. "-It happens sometimes. People just explode. Natural causes."

4. "-You know, I'd almost forgotten what your eyes looked like. Still the same. Pissholes in the snow."

5. "-You can get further with a kind word and a gun than you can with just a kind word."

6. "-It's when you start doing things for free, that you start to grow wings. Isn't that right, Mike.
-What?
-Wings, Michael. You grow wings, and become a fairy."

ANSWER >

1. **DRUGSTORE COWBOY**
1989, USA
Director: Gus Van Sant
Actor: Matt Dillon, Kelly Lynch, James Remar
Script: Gus Van Sant, Daniel Yost and William S. Burroughs.
Based on the book by James Fogle.

2. **BRAVEHEART**
1995, USA
Director: Mel Gibson
Actor: Mel Gibson, Sophie Marceau, Patrick McGoohan
Script: Randall Wallace

3. **REPO MAN**
1984, USA
Director: Alex Cox
Actor: Emilio Estevez, Harry Dean Stanton, Vonetta McGee
Script: Alex Cox

4. **GET CARTER**
1971, UNITED KINGDOM
Director: Mike Hodges
Actor: Michael Caine, Ian Hendry, Britt Ekland
Script: Mike Hodges. Based on the book by Ted Lewis.

5. **THE UNTOUCHABLES**
1987, USA
Director: Brian De Palma
Actor: Kevin Costner, Sean Connery, Charles Martin Smith
Script: David Mamet. Based on the book by Oscar Fraley and Eliot
Ness and Paul Robsky. David Mamet.

6. **MY OWN PRIVATE IDAHO**
1991, USA
Director: Gus Van Sant
Actor: River Phoenix, Keanu Reeves, James Russo
Script: Gus Van Sant

1. "-Do you feel that playing rock 'n' roll music keeps you a child?
That is, keeps you in a state of arrested development?
-No. No. No. I feel it's like, it's more like going, going to a, a
national park or something. And there's, you know, they preserve
the moose. And that's, that's my childhood up there on stage.
That moose, you know.
-So when you're playing you feel like a preserved moose
on stage?
-Yeah."

2. "-Have you been following that man?
-Yeah, I've been following him on my own time.
And anybody can tell I didn't do that to him.
-How?
-Cause he looks too damn good, that's how!"

3. "-Six days does not a week make."

4. "-You're not very bright, are you? I like that in a man."

5. "-It's important to think. It's what separates us from lentils."

6. "-Paulie might have moved slow, but it was only because
Paulie didn't have to move for anybody."

ANSWER >

1. **THIS IS SPINAL TAP**
   1984, USA
   Director: Rob Reiner
   Actor: Michael McKean, Christopher Guest, Harry Shearer
   Script: Christopher Guest, Michael McKean, Rob Reiner and
   Harry Shearer.

2. **DIRTY HARRY**
   1971, USA
   Director: Don Siegal
   Actor: Clint Eastwood, Harry Guardino, Reni Santoni
   Script: Harry Julian Fink, Rita M. Fink, Dean Riesner and John Milius.

3. **BAREFOOT IN THE PARK**
   1967, USA
   Director: Gene Saks
   Actor: Robert Redford, Jane Fonda, Charles Boyer
   Script: Neil Simon

4. **BODY HEAT**
   1981, USA
   Director: Lawrence Kasdan
   Actor: William Hurt, Kathleen Turner, Richard Crenna
   Script: Lawrence Kasdan

5. **THE FISHER KING**
   1991, USA
   Director: Terry Gilliam
   Actor: Robin Williams, Jeff Bridges, Amanda Plummer
   Script: Richard LaGravenese

6. **GOODFELLAS**
   1990, USA
   Director: Martin Scorsese
   Actor: Robert De Niro, Ray Liotta, Joe Pesci
   Script: Nicholas Pileggi and Martin Scorsese.
   Based on the book by Nicholas Pileggi.

1. "-It has been established that persons who have recently died have been returning to life and committing acts of murder."

2. "-We're here to meet a friend. Comin' on the train.
   -Nothin' comin' on the train except a couple of crates and a, uh, coffin!
   -Our friend."

3. "-Last night, Darth Vader came down from planet Vulcan and told me that if I didn't take Lorraine out that he'd melt my brain."

4. "-Nicky's methods of betting weren't scientific, but they worked. When he won, he collected. When he lost, he told the bookies to go fuck themselves. I mean, what were they going to do, muscle Nicky? Nicky was the muscle."

5. "-I must be crazy to be in a loony bin like this."

6. "-I done something new for this fight! I done rassled with a alligator! That's right, I have rassled with a alligator. I done tussled with a whale! I done handcuffed lightning, throwed thunder in jail! That's "bad". Only last week, I murdered a rock, injured a stone, hospitalized a brick. I'm so mean, I make medicine sick!"

ANSWER >

1. NIGHT OF THE LIVING DEAD
    1968, USA
    Director: George A Romero
    Actor: Duane Jones, Judith O'Dea, Russell Streiner
    Script: George A. Romero and John A. Russo.

2. MAD MAX
    1979, AUSTRALIA
    Director: George Miller
    Actor: Mel Gibson, Joanne Samuel, Hugh Keays Byrne
    Script: James McCausland and George Miller.

3. BACK TO THE FUTURE
    1985, USA
    Director: Robert Zemeckis
    Actor: Michael J Fox, Christopher Lloyd, Crispin Glover
    Script: Robert Zemeckis and Bob Gale.

4. CASINO
    1995, USA
    Director: Martin Scorsese
    Actor: Robert De Niro, Sharon Stone Joe Pesci
    Script: Nicholas Pileggi and Martin Scorsese.
    Based on the book by Nicholas Pileggi.

5. ONE FLEW OVER THE CUCKOO'S NEST
    1975, USA
    Director: Milos Forman
    Actor: Jack Nicholson, Louise Fletcher, Brad Dourif
    Script. Bo Goldman and Lawrence Hauben
    Based on the book by Ken Kesey.

6. WHEN WE WERE KINGS
    1996, USA
    Director: Leon Gast
    Actor: Muhammad Ali, George Forman, Don King

1. "-D'you know that the human head weighs 8 pounds?
   -Did you know that Troy Aikman, in only six years, has passed for 16,303 yards?
   -D'you know that bees and dogs can smell fear?
   -Did you know that the career record for hits is 4,256 by Pete Rose who is NOT in the Hall of Fame?
   -D'you know that my next door neighbor has three rabbits?
   -I... I can't compete with that!"

2. "-I don't think I want to know you very well. I don't think you're gonna live much longer."

3. "-All right men, we're on water. I don't want any of you walking to far to the left, or to the right. Remember the training films we saw about how people sink?"

4. "-Tell me something, my friend. You ever dance with the devil by the pale moonlight?"

5. "-She asks me why I'm such a hairy guy."

6. "-Now come on fellas, you wouldn't hit a bloke with no trousers on would you?
   -Alright Charlie, put your trousers on."

ANSWER >

1.   **JERRY MAGUIRE**
     1996, USA
     Director: Cameron Crowe
     Actor: Tom Cruise, Cuba Gooding Jr, Renee Zellweger
     Script: Cameron Crowe

2.   **THREE DAYS OF THE CONDOR**
     1975, USA
     Director: Sydney Pollack
     Actor: Robert Redford, Faye Dunaway, Cliff Robertson
     Script: Lorenzo Semple Jr and David Rayfiel.
     Based on the book by James Grady.

3.   **WHAT'S UP TIGER LILY?**
     1966, JAPAN
     Director: Senkichi Taniguchi
     Actor: Tatsuya Mihashi, Miya Hana, Eiko Wakabayashi
     Script: Woody Allen, Julie Bennett, Frank Buxton, Louise Lasser,
     Len Maxwell, Mickey Rose and Bryan Wilson.

4.   **BATMAN**
     1989, USA
     Director: Tim Burton
     Actor: Jack Nicholson, Michael Keaton, Kim Basinger
     Script: Bob Kane, Sam Hamm and Warren Skaaren.

5.   **HAIR**
     1979, USA
     Director: Milos Forman
     Actor: John Savage, Treat Williams, Beverly D'Angelo
     Script: Gerome Ragni, James Rado, Galt MacDermot and
     Michael Weller.

6.   **THE ITALIAN JOB**
     1969, UNITED KINGDOM
     Director: Peter Collinson
     Actor: Michael Caine, Noel Coward, Maggie Blye
     Script: Troy Kennedy-Martin

1. "-The soul of man has been given wings and at last he is beginning to fly. He is flying into the rainbow! Into the light of hope!"

2. "-Morning Lapoody
   -Morning reverend"

3. "-Impressive. Most impressive. Obi-wan has taught you well. You have controlled your fear. Now, release your anger! Only your hatred can destroy me!"

4. "-I've got a job, a secretary, a mother, two ex-wives and several bartenders dependent upon me, and I don't intend to disappoint them all by getting myself slightly killed."

5. "-What happened to your nose, Gittes? Somebody slammed a bedroom window on it?
   -Nope. Your wife got excited. She crossed her legs a little too quick. You understand what I mean, pal?"

6. "-J.W., this fellow's from England, see, and he's over here workin' with our government, sort of a... secret agent.
   -"Secret Agent"? On whose side?"

ANSWER >

1. **THE GREAT DICTATOR**
   1940, USA
   Director: Charles Chaplin
   Actor: Charles Chaplin, Jack Oakie, Reginald Gardiner
   Script: Charles Chaplin

2. **THE GODS MUST BE CRAZY**
   1980, BOTSWANA
   Director: Jamie Uys
   Actor: Marius Weyers, Sandra Prinsloo, N!xau
   Script: Jamie Uys

3. **THE EMPIRE STRIKES BACK**
   1980, USA
   Director: Irwin Kershner
   Actor: Mark Hamill, Harrison Ford, Carrie Fisher
   Script: George Lucas, Leigh Brackett and Lawrence Kasdan.

4. **NORTH BY NORTHWEST**
   1959, USA
   Director: Alfred Hitchcock
   Actor: Cary Grant, Eva Marie Saint, James Mason
   Script: Ernest Lehman.

5. **CHINATOWN**
   1974, USA
   Director: Roman Polanski
   Actor: Jack Nicholson, Faye Dunaway, John Huston
   Script: Robert Towne and Roman Polanski.

6. **LIVE AND LET DIE**
   1973, UNITED KINGDOM
   Director: Guy Hamilton
   Actor: Roger Moore, Yaphet Kotto, Jane Seymour
   Script: Tom Mankiewicz. Based on the book by Ian Fleming.

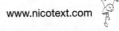

www.nicotext.com

1. "-Hey Bart, it's just me, Charlie
-Really? I hear it's Munt. Madman Munt
-Geez. People can be so cruel. If it's not my build, it's
my personality."

2. "-A census taker once tried to test me. I ate his liver with some
fava beans and a nice Chianti."

3. "-You make it with some of these chicks, they think you gotta
dance with them."

4. "-Well I guess he had it comin'.
-We all got it comin' kid..."

5. "-There's something I've been meaning to ask you for some
time now.
-What's that?
-Can you cure me?
-No. We can care for you, but we can't cure you."

6. "-I find it difficult to convince myself that God would have
introduced such a foul being into creation without endowing
her with some virtues, hmmm?"

ANSWER >

1. **BARTON FINK**
   1991, USA
   Director: Joel Coen
   Actor: John Turturro, John Goodman, Judy Davis
   Script: Ethan Coen and Joel Coen.

2. **THE SILENCE OF THE LAMBS**
   1991, USA
   Director: Jonathan Demme
   Actor: Jodie Foster, Anthony Hopkins, Scott Glenn
   Script: Ted Tally. Based on the book by Thomas Harris.

3. **SATURDAY NIGHT FEVER**
   1977, USA
   Director: John Badham
   Actor: John Travolta, Karen Lynn Gorney, Barry Miller
   Script: Nik Cohn and Norman Wexler.

4. **UNFORGIVEN**
   1992, USA
   Director: Clint Eastwood
   Actor: Clint Eastwood, Gene Hackman, Morgan Freeman
   Script: David Webb Peoples.

5. **THE ELEPHANT MAN**
   1980, USA
   Director: David Lynch
   Actor: Anthony Hopkins, John Hurt, Anne Bancroft
   Script: Christopher De Vore, Eric Bergren and David Lynch.
   Based on the book by Sir Frederick Treves and Ashley Montagu.

6. **THE NAME OF THE ROSE**
   1986, FRANCE/ITALY/WEST-GERMANY
   Director: Jean Jacques Annaud
   Actor: Sean Connery, F Murray Abraham, Christian Slater
   Script: Andrew Birkin, Gérard Brach, Howard Franklin and
   Alain Godard. Based on the book by Umberto Eco.

1. "-Hold on to yourself, Bartlett. You're twenty feet short.
-What do you mean, twenty feet short?
-You're twenty feet short of the woods. The hole is right here out in open. The guard is between us and the lights."

2. "-When I get out, your dead!
-You might be dead before you get out."

3. "-Long people have short faces. Short people have long faces. Big people have little humor, and little people have no humor at all."

4. "-I thrill when I drill a bicuspid / It's swell though they tell me I'm mal-ad-just-ed."

5. "-When it comes to the safety of these people, there's me and then there's God, understand?"

6. "-Wait a minute, Doc. Ah... Are you telling me you built a time machine... out of a DeLorean?
-The way I see it, if you're gonna build a time machine into a car, why not do it with some style?"

ANSWER >

1. THE GREAT ESCAPE
   1962, USA
   Director: John Sturges,
   Actor: Steve McQueen, James Garner, Richard Attenborough
   Script: James Clavell and W.R. Burnett.
   Based on the book by Paul Brickhill.

2. ESCAPE FROM ALCATRAZ
   1979, USA
   Director: Donald Siegel
   Actor: Clint Eastwood, Patrick McGoohan, Roberts Blossom
   Script: Richard Tuggle. Based on the book by J. Campbell Bruce.

3. SINGIN' IN THE RAIN
   1952, USA
   Director: Gene Kelly, Stanley Donen
   Actor: Gene Kelly, Debbie Reynolds, Donald O'Conner
   Script: Betty Comden and Adolph Green.

4. LITTLE SHOP OF HORRORS
   1986, USA
   Director: Frank Oz
   Actor: Rick Moranis, Ellen Greene, Vincent Gardenia
   Script: Charles B. Griffith and Howard Ashman.

5. THE ABYSS
   1989, USA
   Director: James Cameron
   Actor: Ed Harris, Mary Elizabeth Mastrantonio, Michael Biehn
   Script: James Cameron

6. BACK TO THE FUTURE
   1985, USA
   Director: Robert Zemeckis
   Actor: Michael J Fox, Christopher Lloyd, Crispin Glover
   Script: Robert Zemeckis and Bob Gale.

1. "-Why have you disturbed our sleep? Awakened us from our ancient slumber? YOU WILL DIE!!"

2. "-You know what you done there? You told my story. You told my whole story right there, right there. One time, I told you I was gonna make you somebody. That's what you done for me. You made me somebody they're gonna remember."

3. "-Any time you try a decent crime, you got fifty ways you can fuck up. You think of twenty-five of them and you're a genius. And you ain't no genius. You remember who told me that?"

4. "-Ollie, you know my feelings about arming morons: you arm one, you've got to arm them all, otherwise it wouldn't be good sport."

5. "-I move around a lot, not because I'm looking for anything really, but 'cause I'm getting away from things that get bad if I stay."

6. "-I run my unit how I run my unit. You want to investigate me, roll the dice and take your chances. I eat breakfast 300 yards from 4000 Cubans who are trained to kill me, so don't think for one second that you can come down here, flash a badge, and make me nervous."

ANSWER >

1. **THE EVIL DEAD**
   1983, USA
   Director: Sam Raimi
   Actor: Bruce Campbell, Ellen Sandweiss, Hal Delrich
   Script: Sam Raimii

2. **BONNIE AND CLYDE**
   1967, USA
   Director: Arthur Penn
   Actor: Warren Beatty, Faye Dunaway, Michael J Pollard
   Script: David Newman (III), Robert Benton and Robert Towne.

3. **BODY HEAT**
   1981, USA
   Director: Lawrence Kasdan
   Actor: William Hurt, Kathleen Turner, Richard Crenna
   Script: Lawrence Kasdan

4. **NOBODY'S FOOL**
   1994, USA
   Director: Robert Benton
   Actor: Paul Newman, Jessica Tandy, Bruce Willis
   Script: Robert Benton. Based on the book by Richard Russo.

5. **FIVE EASY PIECES**
   1970, USA
   Director: Bob Rafelson
   Actor: Jack Nicholson, Karen Black, Billy Green
   Script: Carole Eastman and Bob Rafelson.

6. **A FEW GOOD MEN**
   1992, USA
   Director: Rob Reiner
   Actor: Tom Cruise, Jack Nicholson, Demi Moore
   Script: Aaron Sorkin and Aaron Sorkin.

1. "-I remember when my daddy gave me that gun. He told me that I should never point it at anything in the house. And that he'd rather I'd shoot at tin cans in the backyard, but he said that sooner or later he supposed the temptation to go after birds would be too much, and that I could shoot all the blue jays I wanted, if I could hit 'em, but to remember it was a sin to kill a mockingbird. Well, I reckon because mockingbirds don't do anything but make music for us to enjoy."

2. "- Never trust a nigger.
   - He could have been white.
   - Never trust anybody."

3. "-I thought I knew you. But I'm not so sure anymore... Do you let anything reach you? I mean, really reach you?"

4. "-I saw Alan this morning and I keep wondering...
   -Alan's in Utah
   - ... And I keep wandering what I was doing in Utah."

5. "-What I can't understand is how you can hit someone six times by accident."

6. "-What are some of your favorite things to do?
   -Well, on Sundays I used to like to go hiking, but now..."

ANSWER >

1. **TO KILL A MOCKINGBIRD**
1962, USA
Director: Robert Mulligan
Actor: Gregory Peck, Mary Badham, Philip Alford
Script: Horton Foote. Based on the book by Harper Lee.

2. **THE FRENCH CONNECTION**
1971, USA
Director: William Friedkin
Actor: Gene Hackman, Fernando Rey, Roy Scheider
Script: Ernest Tidyman, Edward M. Keyes.
Based on the book avRobin Moore.

3. **BULLITT**
1968, USA
Director: Peter Yates
Actor: Steve Mcqueen, Robert Vaughn, Jacqueline Bisset
Script: Alan Trustman and Harry Kleiner.
Based on the book by Robert L. Pike.

4. **FLETCH**
1985, USA
Director: Michael Ritchie
Actor: Chevy Chase, Dana Wheeler Nicholson, Tim Matheson
Script: Andrew Bergman. Based on the book by Gregory McDonald.

5. **FRIED GREEN TOMATOES**
1991, USA
Director: Jon Avnet
Actor: Kathy Bates, Jessica Tandy, Mary Stuart
Script: Carol Sobieski, Fannie Flagg.
Based on the book by Fannie Flagg.

6. **THE BLAIR WITCH PROJECT**
1999, USA
Director: Daniel Myrick, Eduardo Sánchez
Actor: Heather Donahue, Joshua Leonard, Michael C. Williams
Script: Daniel Myrick, Eduardo Sánchez

1. "-Splendid, I thought. What did you think?
   -I, thought, splendid! What did you think?
   -Splendid, I thought."

2. "-You still don't know what you're dealing with do you?
   Perfect organism. Its structural perfection is matched
   only by its hostility."

3. "-If I ever lay my two eyes on you again, I'm gonna walk right
   up to you and hammer on that monkeyed skull of yours 'til it
   rings like a Chinese gong!" '

4. "In the year of our lord thirteen fourteen, patriots of Scotland,
   starving and outnumbered, charged the fields of Bannockburn.
   They fought like warrior poets. They fought like Scotsmen.
   And won their freedom."

5. "-As far back as I can remember, I always wanted
   to be a gangster."

6. "-Truman, I've watched you your whole life. I saw you take your
   first step, your first word, your first kiss. I know you better than
   you know yourself. You're not going to walk out that door...
   -You never had a camera in my head."

ANSWER >

1. **FOUR WEDDINGS AND A FUNERAL**
    1994, UNITED KINGDOM
    Director: Mike Newell
    Actor: Hugh Grant, Andie MacDowell, Kristin Scott
    Script: Richard Curtis

2. **ALIEN**
    1979, USA
    Director: Ridley Scott
    Actor: Tom Skerritt, Sigourney Weaver, John Hurt
    Script: Dan O'Bannon, Ronald Shusett, Dan O'Bannon, David Giler
    and Walter Hill.

3. **HIS GIRL FRIDAY**
    1940, USA
    Director: Howard Hawks
    Actor: Cary Grant, Rosalind Russell, Ralph Bellamy
    Script: Ben Hecht, Charles MacArthur and Charles Lederer.

4. **BRAVEHEART**
    1995, USA
    Director: Mel Gibson
    Actor: Mel Gibson, Sophie Marceau, Patrick McGoohan
    Script: Randall Wallace

5. **GOODFELLAS**
    1990, USA
    Director: Martin Scorsese
    Actor: Robert De Niro, Ray Liotta, Joe Pesci
    Script: Nicholas Pileggi and Martin Scorsese.
    Based on the book by Nicholas Pileggi.

6. **THE TRUMAN SHOW**
    1998, USA
    Director: Peter Weir
    Actor: Jim Carrey, Laura Linney, Ed Harris
    Script: Andrew Niccol.

1. "-Well it's not a train. It's a prison word for... escape.
   But it doesn't stop around here."

2. "-Well, what are you going to do now? Shoot me?
   -No, I don't think so.
   -Then you're going to take these from me? If I could say a
   word about that...
   -No, you can keep them. You can keep as many as you can
   swallow."

3. "-Thank God for the rain to wash the trash off the sidewalk."

4. "-Ya smoke this shit to escape from reality? Me, I don't
   need this shit. I am reality. There's the way it ought to be,
   and there's the way it is."

5. "-The life of the mind. There's no road map for that territory.
   Exploring it can be painful. I have a pain most people don't
   know anything about."

6. "-Protecting the Queen's safety is a task that is gladly accepted
   by Police Squad. No matter how silly the idea of having a queen
   might be to us, as Americans we must be gracious and
   considerate hosts."

ANSWER >

1. **MIDNIGHT EXPRESS**
    1978, UNITED KINGDOM
    Director: Alan Parker
    Actor: Brad Davis, Irene Miracle, Bo Hopkins
    Script: Oliver Stone.
    Based on the book by Billy Hayes and William Hoffer.

2. **MARATHON MAN**
    1976, USA
    Director: John Schlesinger
    Actor: Dustin Hoffman, Laurence Olivier, Roy Scheider
    Script: Robert Towne and William Goldman.
    Based on the book by William Goldman.

3. **TAXI DRIVER**
    1976, USA
    Director: Martin Scorsese
    Actor: Robert De Niro, Cybill Shepherd, Harvey Keitel
    Script: Paul Schrader.

4. **PLATOON**
    1986, USA
    Director: Oliver Stone
    Actor: Tom Berenger, Willem Dafoe, Charlie Sheen
    Script: Oliver Stone

5. **BARTON FINK**
    1991, USA
    Director: Joel Coen
    Actor: John Turturro, John Goodman, Judy Davis
    Script: Ethan Coen and Joel Coen.

6. **THE NAKED GUN:**
    FROM THE FILES OF POLICE SQUAD
    1988, USA
    Director: David Zucker
    Actor: Leslie Nielsen, George Kennedy, Priscilla Presley
    Script: Jim Abrahams, David Zucker and Pat Proft.

1. "-Oh! They've encased him in Carbonite! He should be quite well protected. If he survived the freezing process, that is."

2. "-Hi, Diana Christensen. A racist lackey of the imperialist ruling circles. Laureen Hobbs. Badass commie nigger."

3. "-They're not that different from you, are they? Same haircuts. Full of hormones, just like you. Invincible, just like you feel. The world is their oyster. They believe they're destined for great things, just like many of you, their eyes are full of hope, just like you. Did they wait until it was too late to make from their lives even one iota of what they were capable? Because, you see gentle men, these boys are now fertilizing daffodils. But if you listen real close, you can hear them whisper their legacy to you."

4. "-Love is 2 minutes 55 seconds of squelching noises."

5. "-You are certainly the most distinguished group of highway scofflaws and degenerates ever gathered together in one place"

6. "-You know, the one thing I can't figure out are these girls real smart or real real lucky?
    -Don't matter. Brains'll only get you so far and luck always runs out."

1. **THE EMPIRE STRIKES BACK**
   1980, USA
   Director: Irwin Kershner
   Actor: Mark Hamill, Harrison Ford, Carrie Fisher
   Script: George Lucas, Leigh Brackett and Lawrence Kasdan.

2. **NETWORK**
   1976, USA
   Director: Sidney Lumet
   Actor: William Holden, Faye Dunaway, Peter Finch
   Script: Paddy Chayefsky

3. **DEAD POETS SOCIETY**
   1989, USA
   Director: Peter Weir
   Actor: Robin Williams, Robert Sean Leonard, Ethan Hawke
   Script: Tom Schulman

4. **SID & NANCY**
   1986, USA
   Director: Alex Cox
   Actor: Gary Oldman, Chloe Webb, Drew Schofield
   Script: Alex Cox and Abbe Wool.

5. **THE CANNONBALL RUN**
   1981, USA
   Director: Hal Needham
   Actor: Burt Reynolds, Roger Moore, Farrah Fawcett
   Script: Brock Yates

6. **THELMA & LOUISE**
   1991, USA
   Director: Ridley Scott
   Actor: Susan Sarandon, Geena Davis, Harvey Keitel
   Script: Callie Khouri.

 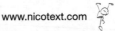

1. "-If you want me to keep my mouth shut, it's gonna cost you some dough. I figure a thousand bucks is reasonable, so I want two."

2. "-The city is made of bricks. The strong make many, the starving make few, the dead make none."

3. "-I am the rocker, I am the roller, I am the out-of-controller!"

4. "-Lobotomy? Isn't that for loonies?
   -Not at all. Friend of mine had one. Designer of the neutron bomb. You ever hear of the neutron bomb? Destroys people - leaves buildings standing. Fits in a suitcase. It's so small, no one knows it's there until - BLAMMO! Eyes melt, skin explodes, everybody dead! So immoral, working on the thing can drive you mad. That's what happened to this friend of mine. So he had a lobotomy. Now he's well again."

5. "-I don't think I've ever drunk champagne before breakfast before. With breakfast on several occasions, but never before, before."

6. "-God is on our side because he hates the Yanks!
   -God is not on our side because he hates idiots also."

ANSWER >

1. **MILLER'S CROSSING**
   1990, USA
   Director: Joel Coen
   Actor: Gabriel Byrne, Albert Finney, Marcia Gay Harden
   Script: Joel Coen and Ethan Coen.
   Based on the book by Dashiell Hammett.

2. **THE TEN COMMANDMENTS**
   1956, USA
   Director: Cecil B Demille
   Actor: Charlton Heston, Yul Brynner, Anne Baxter
   Script: J.H. Ingraham, A.E. Southon, Dorothy Clarke Wilson, Æneas
   MacKenzie, Jesse Lasky Jr., Jack Gariss and Fredric M. Frank.

3. **MAD MAX**
   1979, AUSTRALIEN
   Director: George Miller
   Actor: Mel Gibson, Joanne Samuel, Hugh Keays Byrne
   Script: James McCausland and George Miller.

4. **REPO MAN**
   1984, USA
   Director: Alex Cox
   Actor: Emilio Estevez, Harry Dean Stanton, Vonetta McGee
   Script: Alex Cox

5. **BREAKFAST AT TIFFANY'S**
   1961, USA
   Director: Blake Edwards
   Actor: Audrey Hepburn, George Peppard
   Script: Truman Capote, George Axelrod

6. **THE GOOD, THE BAD, AND THE UGLY**
   1966, ITALY/SPAIN
   Director: Sergio Leone
   Actor: Clint Eastwood, Lee Van Cleef, Eli Wallach
   Script: Luciano Vincenzoni, Sergio Leone, Agenore Incrocci and
   Furio Scarpelli.

1. "-It was one of those days when it's a minute away from snowing and there's this electricity in the air, you can almost hear it. And this bag was, like, dancing with me. Like a little kid begging me to play with it. For fifteen minutes. And that's the day I knew there was this entire life behind things,and... this incredibly benevolent force, that wanted me to know there was no reason to be afraid, ever. Video's a poor excuse. But it helps me remember...and I need to remember... Sometimes there's so much beauty in the world I feel like I can't take it, like my heart's going to cave in."

2. "-You have broken what could not be broken! Hope... is... broken."

3. "-I want to know more about you.
-You already know enough about me. Any more and you're going to get a headache."

4. "-When they send for you, you go in alive, you come out dead, and it's your best friend that does it."

5. "I think I must have one of those faces you can't help believing."

6. "-It's not you marrying me. It's me marrying anyone. I'm mentally. I can't get married to anyone - ever."

ANSWER >

1. AMERICAN BEAUTY
   1999, USA
   Director: Sam Mendes
   Actor: Kevin Spacey, Annette Bening, Thora Birch
   Script: Alan Ball

2. EXCALIBUR
   1981, UNITED KINGDOM
   Director: John Boorman
   Actor: Nicol Williamson, Nigel Terry, Helen Mirren
   Script: Rospo Pallenberg and John Boorman.
   Based on the book by Thomas Malory.

3. XANADU
   1980, USA
   Director: Robert Greenwald
   Actor: Olivia Newton John, Gene Kelly, Michael Beck
   Script: Richard Christian Danus and Marc Reid Rubel.

4. DONNIE BRASCO
   1997, USA
   Director: Mike Newell
   Actor: Al Pacino, Johnny Depp, Michael Madsen
   Script: Paul Attanasio.
   Based on the book by Joseph D. Pistone and Richard Woodley.

5. PSYCHO
   1960, USA
   Director: Alfred Hitchcook
   Actor: Anthony Perkins, Janet Leigh, Vera Miles
   Script: Joseph Stefano. Based on the book by Robert Bland.

6. THE THREE FACES OF EVE
   1957, USA
   Director: Nunnally Johnson
   Actor: Joanne Woodward, David Wayne, Lee J Cobb
   Script: Nunnally Johnson.
   Based on the book by Corbett Thigpen and Hervey M. Cleckley.

1. "-If I asked you to kill me, would you?
-I don't know. How would I do it? I couldn't live without ya"

2. "-Hold me.
-I can't."

3. "-I dunno what the hell's in there, but it's weird and pissed off whatever it is."

4. "-Dave, this conversation can serve no purpose anymore. Goodbye."

5. "-Jane, since I've met you I've noticed things that I never knew were there before; birds singing, dew glistening on a newly formed leaf, stoplights."

6. "-There's no reason to become alarmed, and we hope you'll enjoy the rest of your flight. By the way, is there anyone on board who knows how to fly a plane?"

ANSWER >

1. SID & NANCY
   1986, USA
   Director: Alex Cox
   Actor: Gary Oldman, Chloe Webb, Drew Schofield
   Script: Alex Cox and Abbe Wool.

2. EDWARD SCISSORHANDS
   1990, USA
   Director: Tim Burton
   Actor: Johnny Depp, Winona Ryder, Dianne West
   Script: Tim Burton and Caroline Thompson.

3. THE THING
   1982, USA
   Director: John Carpenter
   Actor: Kurt Russell, Richard Dysart, A Wilford Brimley
   Script: John W. Campbell Jr and Bill Lancaster.

4. 2001: A SPACE ODYSSEY
   1968, UNITED KINGDOM
   Director: Stanley Kubrick
   Actor: Keir Dullea, William Sylvester, Gary Lockwood
   Script: Stanley Kubrick and Arthur C. Clarke.

5. THE NAKED GUN:
   FROM THE FILES OF POLICE SQUAD
   1988, USA
   Director: David Zucker
   Actor: Leslie Nielsen, George Kennedy, Priscilla Presley
   Script: Jim Abrahams, David Zucker and Pat Proft.

6. AIRPLANE! / FLYING HIGH
   1980, USA
   Director: Jim Abrahams, David Zucker, Jerry Zucker
   Actor: Robert Hays, Julie Hagerty, Robert Stack
   Script: Jim Abrahams, David Zucker and Jerry Zucker.

1. "-In Sicily, women are more dangerous than shotguns."

2. "-You don't fuck around with the infinite."

3. "-Do you think God knew what He was doing when He created woman? Huh? No shit. I really wanna know. Or do you think it was another one of His minor mistakes like tidal waves, earth quakes, FLOODS? You think women are like that? What's the matter? You don't think God makes mistakes? Of course He does. We ALL make mistakes. Of course, when WE make mistakes they call it evil. When GOD makes mistakes, they call it... nature. So whaddya think?
   Women... a mistake...or DID HE DO IT TO US ON PURPOSE?"

4. "-Sometimes you have to lose yourself 'fore you can find anything."

5. "I like big fat men like you. When they fall they make more noise!"

6. "-I hear you have a taste for little boys.
   -No Caesar, big boys."

ANSWER >

1. **THE GODFATHER**
   1972, USA
   Director: Francis Ford Coppola
   Actor: Marlon Brando, Al Pacino, James Caan
   Script: Mario Puzo and Francis Ford Coppola.
   Based on the book by Mario Puzo.

2. **MEAN STREETS**
   1973, USA
   Director: Martin Scorsese
   Actor: Robert De Niro, Harvey Keitel, David Proval
   Script: Martin Scorsese and Mardik Martin.

3. **THE WITCHES OF EASTWICK**
   1987, USA
   Director: George Miller
   Actor: Jack Nicholson, Cher, Susan Sarandon
   Script: Michael Cristofer. Based on the book by John Updike.

4. **DELIVERANCE**
   1972, USA
   Director: John Boorman
   Actor: Jon Voight, Burt Reynolds, Ned Beatty
   Script: James Dickey. Based on the book by James Dickey.

5. **THE GOOD, THE BAD, AND THE UGLY**
   1966, ITALY/SPAIN
   Director: Sergio Leone
   Actor: Clint Eastwood, Lee Van Cleef, Eli Wallach
   Script: Luciano Vincenzoni, Sergio Leone, Agenore Incrocci and
   Furio Scarpelli.

6. **CALIGULA**
   1980, ITALY/USA
   Director: Tinto Brass
   Actor: Malcolm McDowell, Peter O'Toole, Teresa Ann Savoy
   Script: Gore Vidal, Bob Guccione, Giancarlo Lui, Masolino D'Amico,
   Franco Rossellini and Roberto Rossellini

www.nicotext.com

1. "-Don't be alarmed, ladies and gentlemen. Those chains are made of chrome steel."

2. "-And you know what they call a... a... a Quarter Pounder with Cheese in Paris?
-They don't call it a Quarter Pounder with cheese?
-No man, they got the metric system. They wouldn't know what the fuck a Quarter Pounder is.
-Then what do they call it?
-They call it a "Royale" with cheese.
-A "Royale" with cheese! What do they call a Big Mac?
-A Big Mac's a Big Mac, but they call it "le Big-Mac".
-"Le Big-Mac"! Ha ha ha ha! What do they call a Whopper?
-I dunno, I didn't go into Burger King."

3. "-Dave...my mind is going...I can feel it...I can feel it."

4. "-You have brought music back in to my life. I had forgotten."

5. "-I'd like to see you with your pants off, Mr. Reed."

6. "-Hi man.
-What are you doing?!
-I'm drinking wine and eating cheese, and catching some rays, you know ..."

ANSWER >

1.   KING KONG
      1976, USA
      Director: John Guillermin
      Actor: Jeff Bridges, Charles Grodin, Jessica Lange
      Script: Merian C. Cooper, Edgar Wallace, James Ashmore
      Creelman, Ruth Rose and Lorenzo Semple Jr.

2.   PULP FICTION
      1994, USA
      Director: Quentin Tarantino
      Actor: John Travolta, Samuel L Jackson, Uma Thurman
      Script: Quentin Tarantino and Roger Avary.

3.   2001: A SPACE ODYSSEY
      1968, UNITED KINGDOM
      Director: Stanley Kubrick
      Actor: Keir Dullea, William Sylvester, Gary Lockwood
      Script: Stanley Kubrick and Arthur C. Clarke.

4.   THE SOUND OF MUSIC
      1965, USA
      Director: Robert Wise
      Actor: Julie Andrews, Christopher Plummer, Eleanor Parker
      Script: Ernest Lehman, Richard Rodgers and Oscar Hammerstein II,
      Howard Lindsay and Russel Crouse.

5.   REDS
      1981, USA
      Director: Warren Beatty
      Actor: Warren Beatty, Diane Keaton, Edward Herrmann
      Script: Warren Beatty, Trevor Griffiths, Elaine May, John Reed (II),
      Jeremy Pikser and Peter S. Feibleman.

6.   KELLY'S HEROES
      1970, USA
      Director: Brian G Hutton
      Actor: Clint Eastwood, Telly Savalas, Don Rickles
      Script: Troy Kennedy-Martin

1. "-This kind of certainty comes but once in a lifetime."

2. "-I only get carsick on boats."

3. "-The best people all shave twice a day."

4. "-Man, I see in fight club the strongest and smartest men who've ever lived. I see all this potential, and I see squandering. God damn it, an entire generation pumping gas, waiting tables; slaves with white collars. Advertising has us chasing cars and clothes, working jobs we hate so we can buy shit we don't need. We're the middle children of history, man. No purpose or place. We have no Great War. No Great Depression. Our Great War's a spiritual war... our Great Depression is our lives. We've all been raised on television to believe that one day we'd all be millionaires, and movie gods, and rock stars. But we won't. And we're slowly learning that fact. And we're very, very pissed off."

5. "-I pray that I may never see the desert again. Hear me, God."

6. "-My idea of Heaven is a solid white nightclub with me as a headliner for all eternity, and they LOVE me."

ANSWER >

1.   THE BRIDGES OF MADISON COUNTY
     1995, USA
     Director: Clint Eastwood
     Actor: Clint Eastwood, Meryl Streep, Annie Corley
     Script: Richard LaGravenese.
     Based on the book avRobert James Waller.

2.   MIDNIGHT COWBOY
     1969, USA
     Director: John Schlesinger
     Actor: Dustin Hoffman, Jon Voight, Sylvia Miles
     Script: Waldo Salt. Based on the book by James Leo Herlihy.

3.   LOLITA
     1962, UNITED KINGDOM
     Director: Stanley Kubrick
     Actor: James Mason, Shelley Winters, Peter Sellers
     Script: Vladimir Nabokov and Stanley Kubrick.
     Based on the book by Vladimir Nabokov.

4.   FIGHT CLUB
     1999, USA
     Director: David Fincher
     Actor: Brad Pitt, Edward Norton, Helena Bonham Carter
     Script: Jim Uhls. Based on the book by Chuck Palahniuk.

5.   LAWRENCE OF ARABIA
     1962, UNITED KINGDOM
     Director: David Lean
     Actor: Peter O'Toole, Alec Guinness, Anthony Quinn
     Script: T.E. Lawrence, Robert Bolt and Michael Wilson.

6.   THE EXORCIST
     1973, USA
     Director: William Friedkin
     Actor: Ellen Burstyn, Max Von Sydow, Linda Blair
     Script: William Peter Blatty

1. "-I've never seen you take a drink in your life.
   -Honey, there are a lot of things you ain't never seen me do,
   that's no sign I don't do 'em."

2. "-The wind opens the sea.
   -God opens the sea with a blast of his nostrils."

3. "-What would you call that hairstyle you're wearing?
   -Arthur."

4. "-At least we've got it stopped.
   -Yeah, as long as the Arctic stays cold."

5. "-I don't want to put a wad of white powder in my nose.
   There's the nasal membrane...
   -You never want to try anything new, Alvy.
   -How can you say that? Whose idea was it? I said that you,
   I and that girl from your acting class should sleep together
   in a threesome.
   -Well, that's sick!
   -Yeah, I know it's sick, but it's new. You didn't say it couldn't
   be sick."

6. "-Boys, you got to learn not to talk to nuns that way."

ANSWER >

1. **THE THREE FACES OF EVE**
   1957, USA
   Director: Nunnally Johnson
   Actor: Joanne Woodward, David Wayne, Lee J Cobb
   Script: Nunnally Johnson.
   Based on the book by Corbett Thigpen and Hervey M. Cleckley.

2. **THE TEN COMMANDMENTS**
   1956, USA
   Director: Cecil B Demille
   Actor: Charlton Heston, Yul Brynner, Anne Baxter
   Script: J.H. Ingraham, A.E. Southon, Dorothy Clarke Wilson, Æneas
   MacKenzie, Jesse Lasky Jr., Jack Gariss and Fredric M. Frank.

3. **A HARD DAY'S NIGHT**
   1964, UNITED KINGDOM
   Director: Richard Lester
   Actor: John Lennon, Paul McCartney, George Harrison
   Script: Alun Owen

4. **THE BLOB**
   1958, USA
   Director:Irwin S. Yeaworth Jr.
   Actor: Steve McQueen, Aneta Corsaut, Earl Rowe
   Script: Kay Linaker, Irwing H. Millgate

5. **ANNIE HALL**
   1977, USA
   Director: Woody Allen
   Actor: Woody Allen, Diane Keaton, Tony Roberts
   Script: Woody Allen and Marshall Brickman.

6. **THE BLUES BROTHERS**
   1980, USA
   Director: John Landis
   Actor: John Belushi, Dan Aykroyd, Cap Calloway
   Script: Dan Aykroyd and John Landis.

1. "-Rhett... If you go ... where shall I go? What shall I do?
   -Frankly, my dear, I don't give a damn."

2. "-This time John Wayne does not walk off into the sunset
   with Grace Kelly.
   -That was Gary Cooper, Asshole."

3. "-Your tongue is old, but sharp, Cicero. Be careful how you wag
   it. One day it will cut off your head."

4. "-So, youw fawtha was a Woman. Who was he?
   -He was a Centurion, in the Jeruselem Garrison.
   -What was his name?
   -Nottius Maximus, sir.
   -Centuwion do you have anyone in your gawwison by that name?
   -No, sir.
   -Well you seem awfully sure, have you checked?
   -I think its a joke, sir. Sort of like...uh...Sillius Sodus,
   or Biggus Dickus."

5. "-The reality is that we do not wash our own laundry...
   It just gets dirtier."

6. "-The richest man is the one with the most powerful friends."

ANSWER >

1. **GONE WITH THE WIND**
   1939, USA
   Director: Victor Fleming
   Actor: Clark Gable, Vivien Leigh, Leslie Howard
   Script: Sidney Howard, Ben Hecht, David O. Selznick, Jo Swerling
   and John Van Druten. Based on the book by Margaret Mitchell.

2. **DIE HARD**
   1988, USA
   Director: John McTiernan
   Actor: Bruce Willis, Alan Rickman, Bonnie Bedelia
   Script: Jeb Stuart and Steven E. de Souza.
   Based on the book by Roderick Thorp.

3. **CLEOPATRA**
   1963, USA
   Director: Joseph L Mankiewicz
   Actor: Elizabeth Taylor, Richard Burton, Rex Harrison
   Script: Sidney Buchman, Ben Hecht, Ranald MacDougall and
   Joseph L. Mankiewicz. Based on the book by Carlo Mario Franzero.

4. **MONTY PYTHON'S LIFE OF BRIAN**
   1979, UNITED KINGDOM
   Director: Terry Jones
   Actor: Graham Chapman, John Cleese, Terry Gilliam
   Script: Graham Chapman, John Cleese, Terry Gilliam, Eric Idle,
   Terry Jones and Michael Palin.

5. **SERPICO**
   1973, USA
   Director: Sidney Lumet
   Actor: Al Pacino, John Randolph, Jack Kehoe
   Script: Waldo Salt and Norman Wexler.
   Based on the book by Peter Maas.

6. **THE GODFATHER PART III**
   1990, USA
   Director: Francis Ford Coppola
   Actor: Al Pacino, Diane Keaton, Talia Shire
   Script: Mario Puzo and Francis Ford Coppola.

1. "-I'd like an omelet, plain, and a chicken salad sandwich on wheat toast, no mayonnaise, no butter, no lettuce. And a cup of coffee.
   -A #2, chicken salad sand. Hold the butter, the lettuce, the mayonnaise, and a cup of coffee. Anything else?
   -Yeah, now all you have to do is hold the chicken, bring me the toast, give me a check for the chicken salad sandwich, and you haven't broken any rules.
   -You want me to hold the chicken, huh?
   -I want you to hold it between your knees."

2. "-Get up, boy. I bet you can squeal. I bet you can squeal like a pig."

3. "-The human spirit is more powerful than any drug - and that's what needs to be nourished."

4. "-Just how bad is it?
   -It's a fire. All fires are bad."

5. "-After all ... tomorrow is another day."

6. "-Monsieur Rick, what kind of a man is Captain Renault?
   -Oh, he's just like any other man, only more so."

ANSWER >

1. FIVE EASY PIECES
    1970, USA
    Director: Bob Rafelson
    Actor: Jack Nicholson, Karen Black, Billy Green
    Script: Carole Eastman and Bob Rafelson.

2. DELIVERANCE
    1972, USA
    Director: John Boorman
    Actor: Jon Voight, Burt Reynolds, Ned Beatty
    Script: James Dickey. Based on the book by James Dickey.

3. AWAKENINGS
    1990, USA
    Director: Penny Marshall
    Actor: Robert De Niro, Robin Williams, Julie Kavner
    Script: Steven Zaillian. Based on the book by Oliver Sacks.

4. THE TOWERING INFERNO
    1974, USA
    Director: John Guillermin, Irwin Allen
    Actor: Steve Mcqueen, Paul Newman, William Holden
    Script: Stirling Silliphant. Based on the book by Richard Martin Stern,
    Thomas N. Scortia and Frank M. Robinson.

5. GONE WITH THE WIND
    1939, USA
    Director: Victor Fleming
    Actor: Clark Gable, Vivien Leigh, Leslie Howard
    Script: Sidney Howard, Ben Hecht, David O. Selznick, Jo Swerling
    and John Van Druten. Based on the book by Margaret Mitchell.

6. CASABLANCA
    1942, USA
    Director: Michael Curtiz
    Actor: Humphrey Bogart, Ingrid Bergman, Paul Henreid
    Script: Murray Burnett, Joan Alison, Julius J. Epstein, Philip G.
    Epstein, Howard K and, Casey Robinson.

www.nicotext.com

1. "-I've been in prison for three years. My dick gets hard if the wind blows."

2. "-I'm tapped out Marv. American Express' got a hit man lookin' for me."

3. "-Have you no human consideration?
-Show me a human, and I might have!"

4. "-Where am I?
-You're in the records room.
-Oh. Do you have the Beatles White Album? Never mind, just bring me a cup of hot fat. And the head of Alfredo Garcia."

5. "-Still wearing your gun on your ankle? Somebody told me the reason you did that was so when you met a chick and rubbed against her she wouldn't know you were a cop. I said that was bullshit. It must be some kind of fast-draw gimmick or something."

6. "-You kill anybody?
-A few cops
-No real people?
-Just cops."

ANSWER >

1. 48HRS
   1982, USA
   Director: Walter Hill
   Actor: Nick Nolte, Eddie Murphy, Annette O'Toole
   Script: Roger Spottiswoode, Walter Hill, Larry Gross,
   Steven E. de Souza and Jeb Stuart.

2. WALL STREET
   1987, USA
   Director: Oliver Stone
   Actor: Michael Douglas, Charlie Sheen, Daryl Hannah
   Script: Stanley Weiser and Oliver Stone.

3. ALL ABOUT EVE
   1950, USA
   Director: Joseph L Mankiewicz
   Actor: Bette Davis, Anne Baxter, George Sanders
   Script: Joseph L. Mankiewicz and Mary Orr.

4. FLETCH
   1985, USA
   Director: Michael Ritchie
   Actor: Chevy Chase, Dana Wheeler Nicholson, Tim Matheson
   Script: Andrew Bergman. Based on the book by Gregory McDonald.

5. THE FRENCH CONNECTION
   1971, USA
   Director: William Friedkin
   Actor: Gene Hackman, Fernando Rey, Roy Scheider
   Script: Ernest Tidyman, Edward M. Keyes.
   Based on the book avRobin Moore.

6. RESERVOIR DOGS
   1992, USA
   Director: Quentin Tarantino
   Actor: Harvey Keitel, Tim Roth, Michael Madsen
   Script: Roger Avary and Quentin Tarantino.

1. "-...and as they both sink beneath the waves, the frog cries out, "Why did you sting me, Mr. Scorpion? For now we both will drown!" Scorpion replies, "I can't help it. It's in my nature!"."

2. "-Winning that ticket, Rose, was the best thing that ever happened to me... it brought me to you. And I'm thankful for that, Rose. I'm thankful. You must do me this honor, Rose. Promise me you'll survive. That you won't give up, no matter what happens, no matter how hopeless. Promise me now, Rose, and never let go of that promise."

3. "-You ever wished you were someone else?
   -I'd like to try being Porky Pig.
   -I never wanted to be anyone else."

4. "-If you want a simple yes or no, you're gonna have to finish the question."

5. "-When your a Jet your a Jet all the way; from your first cigarette until your last dying day!"

6. "-What will we do when we have lost the war?
   -Prepare for the next one."

ANSWER >

1. **THE CRYING GAME**
   1992, UNITED KINGDOM
   Director: Neil Jordan
   Actor: Stephan Rea, Miranda Richardson, Forest Whitaker
   Script: Neil Jordan

2. **TITANIC**
   1997, USA
   Director: James Cameron
   Actor: Leonardo Dicaprio, Kate Winslet, Billy Zane
   Script: James Cameron.

3. **EASY RIDER**
   1969, USA
   Director: Dennis Hopper
   Actor: Peter Fonda, Dennis Hopper, Jack Nicholson
   Script: Peter Fonda, Dennis Hopper and Terry Southern.

4. **BUGSY**
   1991, USA
   Director: Barry Levinson
   Actor: Warren Beatty, Annette Bening, Harvey Keitel
   Script: James Toback. Based on the book by Dean Jennings.

5. **WEST SIDE STORY**
   1961, USA
   Director: Robert Wise, Jerome Robbins
   Actor: Natalie Wood, Richard Beymer, George Chakiris
   Script: Jerome Robbins, Arthur Laurents and Ernest Lehman.
   Based on Romeo and Julia by William Shakespeare.

6. **CROSS OF IRON**
   1977, UNITED KINGDOM/WESTGERMANY
   Director: Sam Peckinpah
   Actor: James Coburn, Maximilian Schell, James Mason
   Script: Julius J. Epstein, James Hamilton and Walter Kelley.
   Based on the book by Frederick Forsyth.

1. "-Is it safe? ...Is it safe?
-You're talking to me?
-Is is safe?
-What safe?
-Is it safe?
-I don't know what you mean. I can't tell you something's safe
or not, unless I know specifically what you're talking about.
-Is it safe?
-Tell me what "it" is first.
-Is it safe?
-Yes, it's safe, it's very safe, so safe you wouldn't believe it.
-Is it safe?
-No, it's not safe, it's very dangerous, be careful."

2. "-He won't get far on hot air and fantasy."

3. "-Let's have an intelligent conversation here: I'll talk,
and you listen."

4. "-Stanley, see this? This is this. This ain't something else,
this is this!"

5. "-A prayer's as good as bayonet on a day like this."

ANSWER >

1. **MARATHON MAN**
    1976, USA
    Director: John Schlesinger
    Actor: Dustin Hoffman, Laurence Olivier, Roy Scheider
    Script: Robert Towne and William Goldman.
    Based on the book by William Goldman.

2. **THE ADVENTURES OF BARON MUNCHAUSEN**
    1989, UNITED KINGDOM
    Director: Terry Gilliam
    Actor: John Neville, Eric Idle, Sarah Polley
    Script: Terry Gilliam and Charles McKeown.
    Based on the book avv Rudolph Erich Raspe.

3. **WATERWORLD**
    1995, USA
    Director: Kevin Reynolds
    Actor: Kevin Costner, Dennis Hopper, Jeanne Tripplehorn
    Script: Peter Rader and David Twohy.

4. **THE DEER HUNTER**
    1978, USA
    Director: Michael Cimino
    Actor: Robert De Niro, Christopher Walken, Meryl Streep
    Script: Michael Cimino, Louis Garfinkle, Quinn K. Redeker and
    Deric Washburn.

5. **ZULU**
    1963, UNITED KINGDOM
    Director: Cy Endfield
    Actor: Stanley Baker, Jack Hawkins, Ulla Jacobsson
    Script: John Prebble, John Prebble and Cy Endfield.

1. "-You can't fight in here, this is the War Room!"

2. "-It means she can't be a witness for us. In fact, when the defense finds her - and they will - she'll be a witness for them!"

3. "-Play it once, Sam. For old times sake.
   -I don't know what you mean, Miss Elsa.
   -Play it, Sam. Play "As time goes by"."

4. "-You said bullshit and experience is all it takes, right?
   Right.
   -Come on in and experience some of my bullshit."

5. "-A guy once told me, "Do not have any attachments, do not have anything in your life you are not willing to walk out on in 30 seconds flat if you spot the heat around the corner."

6. "-Henry, I have some reports here from your Major O'Houlihan that I frankly find hard to believe.
   -Well, don't believe them then, General. Good-bye."

ANSWER >

1. DR STRANGELOVE OR: HOW I LEARNED TO STOP
    WORRYING AND LOVE THE BOMB
    1963, UNITED KINGDOM
    Director: Stanley Kubrick
    Actor: Peter Sellers, George C Scott, Sterling Hayden
    Script: Stanley Kubrick, Terry Southern and Peter George III.
    Based on the book by Peter George.

2. THE ACCUSED
    1988, USA
    Director: Jonathan Kaplan
    Actor: Kelly McGillis, Jodie Foster, Bernie Coulson
    Script: Tom Topor

3. CASABLANCA
    1942, USA
    Director: Michael Curtiz
    Actor: Humphrey Bogart, Ingrid Bergman, Paul Henreid
    Script: Murray Burnett, Joan Alison, Julius J. Epstein, Philip G.
    Epstein, Howard K and, Casey Robinson.

4. 48HRS
    1982, USA
    Director: Walter Hill
    Actor: Nick Nolte, Eddie Murphy, Annette O'Toole
    Script: Roger Spottiswoode, Walter Hill, Larry Gross,
    Steven E. de Souza and Jeb Stuart.

5. HEAT
    1995, USA
    Director: Michael Mann
    Actor: Al Pacino, Robert De Niro, Val Kilmer
    Script: Michael Mann

6. MASH
    1970, USA
    Director: Robert Altman
    Actor: Donald Sutherland, Elliott Gould, Tom Skerritt
    Script: Ring Lardner Jr.
    Based on the book by Richard Hooker.

www.nicotext.com

1. "-Why am I Mr. Pink
   -Cause you're a faggot, that's why!"

2. "-You know...there is really nothing the living can do to bring back
   the dead."

3. "-I don't feel I have to wipe everybody out, Tom.
   Just my enemies."

4. "-We can't bury Cheryl. She's our friend."

5. "-E.T. phone home."

6. "-What kind of childhood did you have?
   -Short."

ANSWER >

1.　　RESERVOIR DOGS
　　　1992, USA
　　　Director: Quentin Tarantino
　　　Actor: Harvey Keitel, Tim Roth, Michael Madsen
　　　Script: Roger Avary and Quentin Tarantino.

2.　　THE TOWERING INFERNO
　　　1974, USA
　　　Director: John Guillermin, Irwin Allen
　　　Actor: Steve Mcqueen, Paul Newman, William Holden
　　　Script: Stirling Silliphant. Based on the book by Richard Martin Stern,
　　　Thomas N. Scortia and Frank M. Robinson.

3.　　THE GODFATHER PART II
　　　1974, USA
　　　Director: Francis Ford Coppola
　　　Actor: Al Pacino, Robert De Niro, Robert Duvall,
　　　Script: Mario Puzo and Francis Ford Coppola.

4.　　THE EVIL DEAD
　　　1983, USA
　　　Director: Sam Raimi
　　　Actor: Bruce Campbell, Ellen Sandweiss, Hal Delrich
　　　Script: Sam Raimi

5.　　E.T THE EXTRA-TERRESTRIAL
　　　1982, USA
　　　Director: Steven Spielberg
　　　Actor: Dee Wallace, Henry Thomas, Peter Coyote
　　　Script: Melissa Mathison

6.　　ESCAPE FROM ALCATRAZ
　　　1979, USA
　　　Director: Donald Siegel
　　　Actor: Clint Eastwood, Patrick McGoohan, Roberts Blossom
　　　Script: Richard Tuggle. Based on the book by J. Campbell Bruce.

1. "-Where the Lord closes a door,
    somewhere He opens a window."

2. "-Well, we went skinny dipping and we did things that frightened
    the fish."

3. "-You're like the thief who isn't the least bit sorry he stole,
    but is terribly, terribly sorry he's going to jail."

4. "-Disturbing the peace? I got thrown out of a window! What's
    the fucking charge for getting pushed out of a moving car, huh?
    Jaywalking?!"

5. "-Martha, in my mind you're buried in cement right up to the
    neck. No, up to the nose, it's much quieter."

6. "-That's the damndest thing I ever saw! I don't know, it seemed
    to swoop down at you deliberately!"

ANSWER >

1. **THE SOUND OF MUSIC**
    1965, USA
    Director: Robert Wise
    Actor: Julie Andrews, Christopher Plummer, Eleanor Parker
    Script: Ernest Lehman, Richard Rodgers and Oscar Hammerstein II,
    Howard Lindsay and Russel Crouse.

2. **STEEL MAGNOLIAS**
    1989, USA
    Director: Herbert Ross
    Actor: Sally Field, Dolly Parton, Julia Roberts
    Script: Robert Harling.

3. **GONE WITH THE WIND**
    1939, USA
    Director: Victor Fleming
    Actor: Clark Gable, Vivien Leigh, Leslie Howard
    Script: Sidney Howard, Ben Hecht, David O. Selznick, Jo Swerling
    and John Van Druten. Based on the book by Margaret Mitchell.

4. **BEVERLY HILLS COP**
    1984, USA
    Director: Martin Brest
    Actor: Eddie Murphy, Judge Reinhold, John Ashton
    Script: Danilo Bach and Daniel Petrie Jr.

5. **WHO'S AFRAID OF VIRGINIA WOOLF**
    1966, USA
    Director: Mike Nichols
    Actor: Elizabeth Taylor, Richard Burton, George Segal
    Script: Edward Albee and Ernest Lehman.

6. **THE BIRDS**
    1963, USA
    Director: Alfred Hitchcock
    Actor: Rod Taylor, Tippi Hedren, Jessica Tandy
    Script: Daphne Du Maurier and Evan Hunter.

1. "-You don't know how hard it is being a woman looking the way I do. You don't know how hard it is being a man looking at the woman looking the way you do."

2. "-There are never enough hours in the days of a queen, and her nights have too many."

3. "-Generally you don't see that kind of behavior in a major appliance."

4. "-If he'd just pay me what he's paying them to stop me robbing him, I'd stop robbing him!"

5. "-A repo man spends his life getting into tense situations."

6. "-Hey, Leatherface, come help me with Grandpa!"

ANSWER >

1. **WHO FRAMED ROGER RABBIT**
   1988, USA
   Director: Robert Zemeckis
   Actor: Bob Hoskins, Christopher Lloyd, Joanna Cassidy
   Script: Jeffrey Price and Peter S. Seaman.
   Based on the book by Gary K. Wolf.

2. **CLEOPATRA**
   1963, USA
   Director: Joseph L Mankiewicz
   Actor: Elizabeth Taylor, Richard Burton, Rex Harrison
   Script: Sidney Buchman, Ben Hecht, Ranald MacDougall and
   Joseph L. Mankiewicz. Based on the book by Carlo Mario Franzero.

3. **GHOSTBUSTERS**
   1984, USA
   Director: Ivan Reitman
   Actor: Bill Murray, Dan Aykroyd, Harold Ramis
   Script: Dan Aykroyd, Harold Ramis and Rick Moranis.

4. **BUTCH CASSIDY AND THE SUNDANCE KID**
   1969, USA
   Director: George Roy Hill
   Actor: Paul Newman, Robert Redford, Katharine Ross
   Script: William Goldman

5. **REPO MAN**
   1984, USA
   Director: Alex Cox
   Actor: Emilio Estevez, Harry Dean Stanton, Vonetta McGee
   Script: Alex Cox

6. **THE TEXAS CHAINSAW MASSACRE**
   1974, USA
   Director: Tobe Hopper
   Actor: Marilyn Burns, Gunner Hansen, Ed Neal
   Script: Kim Henkel and Tobe Hooper.

1. "-Sorry boys, all the stitches in the world can't sew me back together again."

2. "-Henry, I have some reports here from your Major O'Houlihan that I frankly find hard to believe.
   -Well, don't believe them then, General. Good-bye."

3. "-What have you been doing all these years?
   -I've been going to bed early."

4. "-It's Halloween, everyone's entitled to one good scare."

5. "-Meyer, we have known eachother since we were too young to fuck."

6. "-Just because some kid smashes into your wife on the turnpike doesn't make it a crime to be 17."

ANSWER >

1. **CARLITO'S WAY**
   1993, USA
   Director: Brian De Palma
   Actor: Al Pacino, Sean Penn, Penelope Ann Miller
   Script: David Koepp. Based on the book by Edwin Torres.

2. **MASH**
   1970, USA
   Director: Robert Altman
   Actor: Donald Sutherland, Elliott Gould, Tom Skerritt
   Script: Ring Lardner Jr. Based on the book by Richard Hooker.

3. **ONCE UPON A TIME IN AMERICA**
   1984, USA
   Director: Sergio Leone
   Actor: Robert De Niro, James Woods, Elizabeth McGovern
   Script: Leonardo Benvenuti, Piero De Bernardi, Enrico Medioli,
   Franco Arcalli, Franco Ferrini, Sergio Leone, Stuart Kaminsky and
   Ernesto Gastaldi. Based on the book by Harry Grey (II).

4. **HALLOWEEN**
   1978, USA
   Director: John Carpenter
   Actor: Donald Pleasence, Jamie Lee Curtis, Nancy Loomis
   Script: John Carpenter and Debra Hill.

5. **BUGSY**
   1991, USA
   Director: Barry Levinson
   Actor: Warren Beatty, Annette Bening, Harvey Keitel
   Script: James Toback. Based on the book by Dean Jennings.

6. **THE BLOB**
   1958, USA
   Director:Irwin S. Yeaworth Jr.
   Actor: Steve McQueen, Aneta Corsaut, Earl Rowe
   Script: Kay Linaker, Irwing H. Millgate

1. "-Boards don't hit back."

2. "-Hippy, you think everything is a conspiracy.
-Everything is."

3. "-Frankly, you're beginning to smell and for a stud in New York,
that's a handicap."

4. "-Do you believe in God?
-The question is does God believe in me?"

5. "-I know, I know. We are your chosen people. But, once in
a while, can't you choose someone else?"

6. "-Well, I don't like to see things goin' good or bad. I like 'em
in between."

ANSWER >

1. **ENTER THE DRAGON**
   1973, USA
   Director: Robert Clouse
   Actor: Bruce Lee, John Saxon, Jim Kelly
   Script: Michael Allin

2. **THE ABYSS**
   1989, USA
   Director: James Cameron
   Actor: Ed Harris, Mary Elizabeth Mastrantonio, Michael Biehn
   Script: James Cameron

3. **MIDNIGHT COWBOY**
   1969, USA
   Director: John Schlesinger
   Actor: Dustin Hoffman, Jon Voight, Sylvia Miles
   Script: Waldo Salt. Based on the book by James Leo Herlihy.

4. **LOLITA**
   1962, UNITED KINGDOM
   Director: Stanley Kubrick
   Actor: James Mason, Shelley Winters, Peter Sellers
   Script: Vladimir Nabokov and Stanley Kubrick.
   Based on the book by Vladimir Nabokov.

5. **FIDDLER ON THE ROOF**
   1971, USA
   Director: Norman Jewison
   Actor: (Chaim) Topol, Norma Crane, Leonard Frey
   Script: Joseph Stein. Based on the book by Sholom Aleichem.

6. **RED RIVER**
   1948, USA
   Director: Howard Hawks
   Actor: John Wayne, Montgomery Clift, Walter Brennan
   Script: Borden Chase, Borden Chase and Charles Schnee

1. "-I do wish we could chat longer, but I'm having an old friend for dinner. Bye."

2. "-Is this where you live?
   -Who lives?"

3. "-I'm the best you ever seen Fats. I'm the best there is. Even if you beat me I'm still the best."

4. "-That's too bad. I was going to marry her. I already put a deposit on twin cemetery plots."

5. "-It only took me one night to realize that if brains were dynamite, you couldn't even blow your nose."

6. "-Never. I'll never turn to the Dark Side. You've failed, your highness. I am a Jedi, like my father before me."

ANSWER >

1. **THE SILENCE OF THE LAMBS**
   1991, USA
   Director: Jonathan Demme
   Actor: Jodie Foster, Anthony Hopkins, Scott Glenn
   Script: Ted Tally. Based on the book by Thomas Harris.

2. **REBEL WITHOUT A CAUSE**
   1955, USA
   Director: Nicholas Ray
   Actor: James Dean, Natalie Wood, Sal Mineo
   Script: Nicholas Ray, Irving Shulman and Stewart Stern.

3. **THE HUSTLER**
   1961, USA
   Director: Robert Rossen
   Actor: Paul Newman, Jackie Gleason, Piper Lauire
   Script: Sidney Carroll and Robert Rossen.
   Based on the book by Walter Tevis.

4. **WHAT'S UP TIGER LILY?**
   1966, JAPAN
   Director: Senkichi Taniguchi
   Actor: Tatsuya Mihashi, Miya Hana, Eiko Wakabayashi
   Script: Woody Allen, Julie Bennett, Frank Buxton, Louise Lasser, Len
   Maxwell, Mickey Rose and Bryan Wilson.

5. **AMERICAN GRAFFITI**
   1973, USA
   Director: George Lucas
   Actor: Richard Dreyfuss, Ronny Howard, Paul LeMat
   Script: George Lucas, Gloria Katz and Willard Huyck.

6. **RETURN OF THE JEDI**
   1983, USA
   Director: Richard Marquand
   Actor: Mark Hamill, Harrison Ford, Carrie Fisher
   Script: George Lucas and Lawrence Kasdan.

1. "-How do you feel?
   -Like the kling klang king of the rim ram room."

2. "-The only arithmetic he ever got was hearing the referee
   count up to ten."

3. "-He's more machine now than man; twisted and evil."

4. "-Excuse me, Are the voices inside my head bothering you?"

5. "-Seven schools in seven states and the only thing different
   is my locker combination."

6. "-You give me powders, pills, baths, injections,
   enemas when all I need is love."

ANSWER >

1.   LEAVING LAS VEGAS
      1995, USA
      Director: Mike Figgis
      Actor: Nicolas Cage, Elisabeth Shue, Julian Sands
      Script: Mike Figgis. Based on the book by John O'Brien.

2.   WATERFRONT
      1950 UNITED KINGDOM
      Director: Michael Anderson
      Actor: Robert Newton, Kathleen Harrison
      Script: John Brophy, Paul Soskin

3.   RETURN OF THE JEDI
      1983, USA
      Director: Richard Marquand
      Actor: Mark Hamill, Harrison Ford, Carrie Fisher
      Script: George Lucas and Lawrence Kasdan.

4.   THE GODS MUST BE CRAZY
      1980, BOTSWANA
      Director: Jamie Uys
      Actor: Marius Weyers, Sandra Prinsloo, N!xau
      Script: Jamie Uys

5.   HEATHERS
      1989, USA
      Director: Michael Lehmann
      Actor: Winona Ryder, Christian Slater, Shannen Doherty
      Script: Daniel Waters

6.   THE BRIDGE ON THE RIVER KWAI
      1957, UNITED KINGDOM
      Director: David Lean
      Actor: William Holden, Alec Guinness, Jack Hwakins
      Script: Michael Wilson, Carl Foreman.
      Based on the book by Pierre Boulle.

1. "-I'm just a sweet transvestite, from Transsexual Transylvania."

2. "-Sometimes I don't know where the bullshit ends and the truth begins."

3. "-First learn stand...then learn fly...nature's rule..Daniel-san, not mine."

4. "-Now listen to me, all of you. You are all condemned men. We keep you alive to serve this ship. So row well, and live."

5. "-There's been a lamp burning in the window for ya, honey.
   -No thanks, I jumped out that window a long time ago."

6. "-I'm going next. So if ole' fat ass gets stuck, I won't get stuck behind her!"

ANSWER >

1. THE ROCKY HORROR PICTURE SHOW
   1975, USA
   Director: Jim Sharman
   Actor: Tim Curry, Susan Sarandon, Barry Bostwick
   Script: Richard O'Brien, Jim Sharman

2. ALL THAT JAZZ
   1979, USA
   Director: Bob Fosse
   Actor: Roy Schneider, Jessica Lange, Ann Reinking
   Script: Robert Alan Aurthur and Bob Fosse.

3. THE KARATE KID
   1984, USA
   Director: John G Avildsen
   Actor: Ralph Macchio, Noriyuki Morita, Elisabeth Shue
   Script: Robert Mark Kamen

4. BEN-HUR
   1959, USA
   Director: William Wyler
   Actor: Charlton Heston, Jack Hawkins, Stephen Boyd
   Script: Karl Tunberg, Maxwell Anderson, Christopher Fry and
   Gore Vidal. Based on the book by Lew Wallace.

5. HIS GIRL FRIDAY
   1940, USA
   Director: Howard Hawks
   Actor: Cary Grant, Rosalind Russell, Ralph Bellamy
   Script: Ben Hecht, Charles MacArthur and Charles Lederer.

6. THE POSEIDON ADVENTURE
   1972, USA
   Director: Ronald Neame
   Actor: Gene Hackman, Ernest Borgnine, Red Buttons
   Script: Wendell Mayes and Stirling Silliphant.
   Based on the book by Paul Gallico.

1. "-Just when I thought that I was out they pull me back in."

2. "-Which one of you nuts has got any guts?"

3. "-No matter what anybody tells you, words and ideas can change the world."

4. "-All those moments will be lost in time, like tears in rain."

5. "-Don't kid yourself, Francesca: you are anything but a simple woman."

6. "-I'm young, I'm handsome, I'm fast, I'm pretty and can't possibly be beat."

ANSWER >

1.   THE GODFATHER PART III
        1990, USA
        Director: Francis Ford Coppola
        Actor: Al Pacino, Diane Keaton, Talia Shire
        Script: Mario Puzo and Francis Ford Coppola.

2.   ONE FLEW OVER THE CUCKOO'S NEST
        1975, USA
        Director: Milos Forman
        Actor: Jack Nicholson, Louise Fletcher, Brad Dourif
        Script. Bo Goldman and Lawrence Hauben
        Based on the book by Ken Kesey.

3.   DEAD POETS SOCIETY
        1989, USA
        Director: Peter Weir
        Actor: Robin Williams, Robert Sean Leonard, Ethan Hawke
        Script: Tom Schulman

4.   BLADE RUNNER
        1982, USA
        Director: Ridley Scott
        Actor: Harrison Ford, Rutger Hauer, Sean Young
        Script: Hampton Fancher, David Webb Peoples, Roland Kibbee.
        Based on the book by Philip K. Dick.

5.   THE BRIDGES OF MADISON COUNTY
        1995, USA
        Director: Clint Eastwood
        Actor: Clint Eastwood, Meryl Streep, Annie Corley
        Script: Richard LaGravenese.
        Based on the book avRobert James Waller.

6.   WHEN WE WERE KINGS
        1996, USA
        Director: Leon Gast
        Actor: Muhammad Ali, George Forman, Don King

1. "-Might as well call it white jack!"

2. "-That's funny, that plane's dustin' crops where there ain't no crops."

3. "-Top o' the world ma....top o' the world."

4. "-When a man says no to champagne, he says no to life."

5. "-Well, I'm sure I'd feel much worse if I weren't under such heavy sedation."

6. "-Toto, I've a feeling we're not in Kansas anymore."

ANSWER >

1. **OCEAN'S ELEVEN**
   1960, USA
   Director: Lewis Milestone
   Actor: Frank Sinatra, Dean Martin, Sammy Davis Jr
   Script: George Clayton Johnson, Jack Golden Russell, Harry Brown, Charles Lederer and Billy Wilder.

2. **NORTH BY NORTHWEST**
   1959, USA
   Director: Alfred Hitchcock
   Actor: Cary Grant, Eva Marie Saint, James Mason
   Script: Ernest Lehman.

3. **WHITE HEAT**
   1949, USA
   Director: Raoul Walsh
   Actor: James Cagney, Virginia Mayo, Edmond O'Brien
   Script: Virginia Kellogg, Ivan Goff and Ben Roberts.

4. **THE DEER HUNTER**
   1978, USA
   Director: Michael Cimino
   Actor: Robert De Niro, Christopher Walken, Meryl Streep
   Script: Michael Cimino, Louis Garfinkle, Quinn K. Redeker and Deric Washburn.

5. **THIS IS SPINAL TAP**
   1984, USA
   Director: Rob Reiner
   Actor: Michael McKean, Christopher Guest, Harry Shearer
   Script: Christopher Guest, Michael McKean, Rob Reiner and Harry Shearer.

6. **THE WIZARD OF OZ**
   1939, USA
   Director: Victor Fleming
   Actor: Judy Garland, Ray Bolger, Bert Lahr
   Script: Noel Langley, Florence Ryerson and Edgar Allan Woolf.
   Based on the book by L. Frank Baum.

1.   "-There's nothing more life-affirming than getting the shit
      kicked outta ya'."

2.   "-I'm a spoke on a wheel. I am, and so are you."

3.   "-Twenty dwarves took turns doing handstands on the carpet."

4.   "-Sweetheart, you can't buy the necessities of life with cookies."

5.   "-They asked me if I'd seen any strangers in the neighborhood."

6.   "-You get what you settle for."

ANSWER >

1.   DRUGSTORE COWBOY
     1989, USA
     Director: Gus Van Sant
     Actor: Matt Dillon, Kelly Lynch, James Remar
     Script: Gus Van Sant, Daniel Yost and William S. Burroughs.
     Based on the book by James Fogle.

2.   DONNIE BRASCO
     1997, USA
     Director: Mike Newell
     Actor: Al Pacino, Johnny Depp, Michael Madsen
     Script: Paul Attanasio.
     Based on the book by Joseph D. Pistone and Richard Woodley.

3.   BUGSY
     1991, USA
     Director: Barry Levinson
     Actor: Warren Beatty, Annette Bening, Harvey Keitel
     Script: James Toback. Based on the book by Dean Jennings.

4.   EDWARD SCISSORHANDS
     1990, USA
     Director: Tim Burton
     Actor: Johnny Depp, Winona Ryder, Dianne West
     Script: Tim Burton and Caroline Thompson.

5.   CLOSE ENCOUNTERS OF THE THIRD KIND
     1977, USA
     Director: Steven Spielberg
     Actor: Richard Dreyfuss, Francois Truffaut, Teri Garr
     Script: Steven Spielberg, Hal Barwood, Jerry Belson, John Hill and
     Matthew Robbins.

6.   THELMA & LOUISE
     1991, USA
     Director: Ridley Scott
     Actor: Susan Sarandon, Geena Davis, Harvey Keitel
     Script: Callie Khouri.

1. "-Nothing more foolish than a man chasin' his hat."

2. "-God made men. Men made slaves."

3. "-This whole world's wild at heart and weird on top."

4. "-I'll never look like Barbie. Barbie doesn't have bruises."

5. "The only thing I'll ever lay is a rug!"

6. "-The Force can have a strong influence on a weak mind."

ANSWER >

1. **MILLER'S CROSSING**
   1990, USA
   Director: Joel Coen
   Actor: Gabriel Byrne, Albert Finney, Marcia Gay Harden
   Script: Joel Coen and Ethan Coen.
   Based on the book by Dashiell Hammett.

2. **THE TEN COMMANDMENTS**
   1956, USA
   Director: Cecil B Demille
   Actor: Charlton Heston, Yul Brynner, Anne Baxter
   Script: J.H. Ingraham, A.E. Southon, Dorothy Clarke Wilson, Æneas
   MacKenzie, Jesse Lasky Jr., Jack Gariss and Fredric M. Frank.

3. **WILD AT HEART**
   1990, USA
   Director: David Lynch
   Actor: Nicolas Cage, Laura Dern, Diane Ladd
   Script: David Lynch. Based on the book by Barry Gifford.

4. **SID & NANCY**
   1986, USA
   Director: Alex Cox
   Actor: Gary Oldman, Chloe Webb, Drew Schofield
   Script: Alex Cox and Abbe Wool.

5. **ROCK 'N' ROLL HIGH SCHOOL**
   1979, USA
   Director: Allan Arkush, Joe Dante
   Actor: P.J Soles, Vincent van Patten, Clint Howard
   Script: Richard Whitley, Russ Dronch

6. **STAR WARS**
   1977, USA
   Director: George Lucas
   Actor: Mark Hamill, Harrison Ford, Carrie Fisher
   Script: George Lucas

1. "-The best goodbyes are short. Adieu."

2. "-I'm too old for this shit!"

3. "-In case I forget to tell you later, I had a really good time tonight."

4. "-I swear to GOD George, if you ever EXISTED I'd divorce you."

5. "-Just like a Wop to bring a knife to a gunfight."

6. "-In Rome, dignity shortens life even more surely than disease."

ANSWER >

1. **THE MALTESE FALCON**
   1941, USA
   Director: John Huston
   Actor: Humphrey Bogart, Mary Astor, Peter Lorre
   Script: John Huston. Based on the book by Dashiell Hammett.

2. **LETHAL WEAPON**
   1987, USA
   Director: Richard Donner
   Actor: Mel Gibson, Danny Glover, Gary Busey
   Script: Shane Black

3. **PRETTY WOMAN**
   1990, USA
   Director: Garry Marshall
   Actor: Richard Gere, Julia Roberts, Ralph Bellamy
   Script: J.F Lawton

4. **WHO'S AFRAID OF VIRGINIA WOOLF**
   1966, USA
   Director: Mike Nichols
   Actor: Elizabeth Taylor, Richard Burton, George Segal
   Script: Edward Albee and Ernest Lehman.

5. **THE UNTOUCHABLES**
   1987, USA
   Director: Brian De Palma
   Actor: Kevin Costner, Sean Connery, Charles Martin Smith
   Script: David Mamet. Based on the book by Oscar Fraley and Eliot Ness and Paul Robsky. David Mamet.

6. **SPARTACUS**
   1960, USA
   Director: Stanley Kubrick
   Actor: Kirk Douglas, Laurence Olivier, Jean Simmons
   Script: Dalton Trumbo, Calder Willingham and Peter Ustinov. Based on the book by Howard Fast.

1.   "-We seem to be made to suffer. It's our lot in life."

2.   "-Pain can be controlled, you just disconnect it."

3.   "I'm just a mean green mother from outer space and I'm bad!"

4.   "-Uh, well, sir, I ain't a real cowboy. But I am one helluva stud!"

5.   "-You are the Duke of New York! You're A Number 1!"

6.   "-I heard someone screaming, and it was me."

ANSWER >

1. **STAR WARS**
   1977, USA
   Director: George Lucas
   Actor: Mark Hamill, Harrison Ford, Carrie Fisher
   Script: George Lucas

2. **THE TERMINATOR**
   1984, USA
   Director: James Cameron
   Actor: Arnold Schwartzenegger, Michael Biehn,
   Linda Hamilton Script: James Cameron, Gale Anne Hurd,
   William Wisher Jr and Harlan Ellison.

3. **LITTLE SHOP OF HORRORS**
   1986, USA
   Director: Frank Oz
   Actor: Rick Moranis, Ellen Greene, Vincent Gardenia
   Script: Charles B. Griffith and Howard Ashman.

4. **MIDNIGHT COWBOY**
   1969, USA
   Director: John Schlesinger
   Actor: Dustin Hoffman, Jon Voight, Sylvia Miles
   Script: Waldo Salt. Based on the book by James Leo Herlihy.

5. **ESCAPE FROM NEW YORK**
   1981, USA
   Director: John Carpenter
   Actor: Kurt Russell, Lee Van Cleef, Ernest Borgnine
   Script: John Carpenter and Nick Castle.

6. **THE ACCUSED**
   1988, USA
   Director: Jonathan Kaplan
   Actor: Kelly McGillis, Jodie Foster, Bernie Coulson
   Script: Tom Topor

1. "-He knew the risks, he didn't have to be there. It rains...
   you get wet."

2. "-You know what the Queen said? If I had balls, I'd be King."

3. "-Some places are like people: some shine and some don't."

4. "-When they come...they come at what you love."

5. "-Wax on, wax off..."

6. "-Divine decadence darling!"

ANSWER >

1.   HEAT
      1995, USA
      Director: Michael Mann
      Actor: Al Pacino, Robert De Niro, Val Kilmer
      Script: Michael Mann

2.   MEAN STREETS
      1973, USA
      Director: Martin Scorsese
      Actor: Robert De Niro, Harvey Keitel, David Proval
      Script: Martin Scorsese and Mardik Martin.

3.   THE SHINING
      1980, USA
      Director: Stanley Kubrick
      Actor: Jack Nicholson, Shelley Duvall, Danny Lloyd
      Script: Stanley Kubrick and Diane Johnson.
      Based on the book by Stephen King.

4.   THE GODFATHER PART III
      1990, USA
      Director: Francis Ford Coppola
      Actor: Al Pacino, Diane Keaton, Talia Shire
      Script: Mario Puzo and Francis Ford Coppola.

5.   THE KARATE KID
      1984, USA
      Director: John G Avildsen
      Actor: Ralph Macchio, Noriyuki Morita, Elisabeth Shue
      Script: Robert Mark Kamen

6.   CABARET
      1972, USA
      Director: Bob Fosse
      Actor: Liza Minelli, Michael York, Helmut Griem
      Script: John Van Druten, Joe Masteroff, Jay Presson Allen and
      Hugh Wheeler. Based on the book by Christopher Isherwood.

1. "-Play it cool boy, real cool."

2. "-Get busy living, or get busy dying. That's goddamn right."

3. "-What'd the old man trade for those guys, a used puck bag?"

4. "-You're tearing me apart!"

5. "-It ain't like it used to be, but it'll do."

6. "-They laughed at me, Mama."

ANSWER >

1. **WEST SIDE STORY**
   1961, USA
   Director: Robert Wise, Jerome Robbins
   Actor: Natalie Wood, Richard Beymer, George Chakiris
   Script: Jerome Robbins, Arthur Laurents and Ernest Lehman.
   Based on Romeo and Julia by William Shakespeare.

2. **THE SHAWSHANK REDEMPTION**
   1994, USA
   Director: Frank Darabont
   Actor: Tim Robbins, Morgan Freeman, Bob Gunton
   Script: Frank Darabont. Based on the book by Stephen King.

3. **SLAP SHOT**
   1977, USA
   Director: George Roy
   Actor: Paul Newman, Michael Ontkean, Lindsay Crouse
   Script: Nancy Dowd

4. **REBEL WITHOUT A CAUSE**
   1955, USA
   Director: Nicholas Ray
   Actor: James Dean, Natalie Wood, Sal Mineo
   Script: Nicholas Ray, Irving Shulman and Stewart Stern.

5. **THE WILD BUNCH**
   1969, USA
   Director: Sam Peckinpah
   Actor: William Holden, Ernest Borgnine, Robert Ryan
   Script: Walon Green, Roy N. Sickner, Walon Green and
   Sam Peckinpah.

6. **CARRIE**
   1976, USA
   Director: Brian De Palma
   Actor: Sissy Spacek, Piper Laurie, William Katt
   Script: Lawrence D. Cohen. Based on the book by Stephen King.

1. "-Cyborgs don't feel pain. I do. Don't do that again."

2. "-To be on the wire is life. The rest is waiting."

3. "-I would like if I may to take you on a strange journey."

4. "-Have you had a close encounter?"

5. "-Now take that underwear off your head. Enough's enough."

6. "-Rockin' good news."

ANSWER >

1. **THE TERMINATOR**
   1984, USA
   Director: James Cameron
   Actor: Arnold Schwartzenegger, Michael Biehn,
   Linda Hamilton
   Script: James Cameron, Gale Anne Hurd, William Wisher Jr and
   Harlan Ellison.

2. **ALL THAT JAZZ**
   1979, USA
   Director: Bob Fosse
   Actor: Roy Schneider, Jessica Lange, Ann Reinking
   Script: Robert Alan Aurthur and Bob Fosse.

3. **THE ROCKY HORROR PICTURE SHOW**
   1975, USA
   Director: Jim Sharman
   Actor: Tim Curry, Susan Sarandon, Barry Bostwick
   Script: Richard O'Brien, Jim Sharman

4. **CLOSE ENCOUNTERS OF THE THIRD KIND**
   1977, USA
   Director: Steven Spielberg
   Actor: Richard Dreyfuss, Francois Truffaut, Teri Garr
   Script: Steven Spielberg, Hal Barwood, Jerry Belson, John Hill and
   Matthew Robbins.

5. **KELLY'S HEROES**
   1970, USA
   Director: Brian G Hutton
   Actor: Clint Eastwood, Telly Savalas, Don Rickles
   Script: Troy Kennedy-Martin

6. **WILD AT HEART**
   1990, USA
   Director: David Lynch
   Actor: Nicolas Cage, Laura Dern, Diane Ladd
   Script: David Lynch. Based on the book by Barry Gifford.

www.nicotext.com

Index

Index

Index

Index

Index